Critics praised Susan Trott's national bestseller *The Holy Man* as "endlessly entertaining and gently profound" (*Kirkus Reviews*). "With wit and modern insight, it compels readers to look inward, to turn to themselves, for enlightenment" (*Booklist*). Now Trott continues her entertaining and spiritually illuminating tales of the holy man with *The Holy Man's Journey*.

The holy man undertakes a pilgrimage of his own to find his old teacher. He must leave his beloved hermitage and fellow monks, perhaps never to return. Accompanying him is his student successor, Anna, who among other lessons on the road with the holy man, learns that by giving, one can prevent stealing, by taking blame, one can remain innocent, and by asking for assistance, one can offer help.

Intimate and revealing, this is a tale of friendship and love that shows the human side of the holy man while never ceasing to instruct and enlighten the reader.

THE
HOLY
MAN'S
JOURNEY

SUSAN
TROTT

RIVERHEAD BOOKS

New York

Riverhead Books
Published by The Berkley Publishing Group
A member of Penguin Putnam Inc.
200 Madison Avenue
New York, New York 10016

Copyright © 1997 by Susan Trott
Book design by Marysarah Quinn
Cover design by Lisa Amoroso
Cover illustration by James Barkley

First Riverhead hardcover edition: March 1997
First Riverhead trade paperback edition: April 1998
Riverhead trade paperback ISBN: 1-57322-660-2

The Penguin Putnam Inc. World Wide Web site address is http://www.penguinputnam.com

The Library of Congress has catalogued the Riverhead hardcover edition as follows:

Trott, Susan.
The holy man's journey / by Susan Trott.
p.   cm.
ISBN: 1-57322-057-4
I. Title
PS3570.R594H59   1997   96-48653 CIP
813'.54—dc21

Printed in the United States of America

10 9 8 7 6 5 4 3 2 1

to my grandchildren:
Alexandra Mitchell, Walker Ryan, Rosalie Ryan,
with thanks to Rosalie for the picture
of the holy man

CONTENTS

THE HOLY MAN'S JOURNEY

1
BEING A ROCK

Spring came to the holy man's hermitage. The mountain was awash with water. It sang with the sound of rivulets, streams, creeks, and cataracts, all rushing to the reservoir in the town ten miles below. The wild iris began to shyly appear, pale lilac, the color of the melting snow itself and of the mountain light just before dawn.

The boulder birds returned, looking a bit straggly and stunned as if having flown through a tempest, but happy to find home boulders to alight on at last, and sing a song about. The steady rocks were paradise after the long wind-tossed, rain-jostled journey from the south.

The holy man wandered around, looking a bit stunned himself, surprised to be around to greet another spring on his beloved mountain. Just when things had looked their worst during the hard winter months, when his heart, physically and metaphorically, was giving out, Anna had appeared with her husband and children to nurse him back to health. Jacob, the pilgrim who had been a killer but was now redeemed, had found them in Dublin and brought them to the hermitage as a gift to the holy man. The greatest part of it was the sound of the children's laughter, which encouraged Joe to hang on to life a little longer so he could pass on his wisdom to Anna, his chosen one.

Joe wandered about the boulder garden and greeted the returning birds who alit on him as well as the boulders, not because he was the holy man—they didn't know that—but because something about Joe was like a rock: steady and safe, one with the ground and the air, warmed by the sun, celebrating the wind and rain, this although he was a small, frail, plain-looking man of seventy-three years.

Joe stood still for a long time when a boulder bird came to him. It was something he could do well and yet another thing he must remember to teach Anna before he died; to be still. But Anna was watching from the window and already learning. She rarely took her eyes off the holy man, because she knew it was her job now to be learning from him and, anyhow, there was nothing she would rather do than be with Joe and try to do as he did.

Motionless, he was a rock for an hour, with birds on his head and shoulders and one on his foot, all of them coming and going but mostly staying. While in this posture, he watched the clouds move across the sky. He saw a beetle stroll along the ground, six tiny alternating steps at a time, and disappear into the new green spears of grass near the spring. Two small blue butterflies whirled around each other in an intricate aerial dance, while a yellow one wafted aimlessly, making patterns in the air.

Joe was having a wonderful time, but when one of the birds returned to his shoulder with a small twig in his beak, he figured it was time to stop being a rock. Good though he was at remaining still for long periods, he could not pause for the term it would take for the bird to build a nest, lay her eggs, hatch them, and teach the chicks to fly.

No, Joe thought, I don't have that much time left and there are a few things I must attend to that are almost as important as being rock and nest-bearer.

Slowly he began to stir so that the birds thought it was their own idea to remove themselves from him, and not that Joe was unperching them. He did not want to instill in them the slightest doubt of the immovability and safe-haven-ness of rocks in general.

At the window, Anna was joined by Jimmy, her five-year-old son. "What is Joe doing?" he asked.

"Being a rock, I think."

Jimmy watched for a while. "Can we be rocks?"

"Sure," she said. "We can be anything."

He took her hand excitedly. "Let's go."

To Anna, that "let's go" contained all the thrill of childhood. It was the exalted cry that the holy man wanted to hear from people of all ages, expressing the excitement of life's possibilities on every given day.

Although Anna knew the outlook wasn't good for her and Jimmy to be unwiggly rocks, they ran out to the boulder garden to try.

2
DRAMA

Jimmy was five years old, peaceful and thoughtful, physically strong, humorous and inventive. Melissa was three and a half, full of fun and imagination, a strong-minded individual. Both were kind and loving like their mother. Their father, Errol, was an intelligent, strong, capable person, an architect by profession, also kind and loving but plagued, Joe thought, by restlessness and dissatisfaction.

Errol found the hermitage to be confining in the extreme. Over the winter months, he had often gone snowshoeing on the trackless mountain, filling his family with fear. He would return exhilarated but several times had to be saved by Jacob who, being from the European Alps, was familiar with the wiles of ice and snow, unlike the lowland Irish Errol. Once, lost in a whiteout, Errol spent three days in a snow cave and almost died. His adventurousness and love of drama led to irresponsibility but added to his charm. He was a captivating person.

That spring night was particularly cold, and a rain storm driven by a northeast wind swirled around the hermitage. Errol had not returned by dark. Jacob was still unwell from the long, weary tracking of Errol the last time he was lost and so could not go and look for the errant husband's trail. Joe urged Anna and the children, who were tired and anxious, to go to bed. "He is all right. I promise you. He will soon be home. I will wait up for him and have some hot potato soup ready."

Anna did what the holy man enjoined her to. Soon Joe heard bedtime stories and lullabies from the next room. Until summer, and the arrival of the monks, they were using only the bottom floor so her family slept in the common room, Jacob in the study, and Joe in the kitchen, all on mattresses taken from the beds in the rooms above.

Joe sat peacefully and waited. Around midnight, there was a clawing at the door, a muffled call. Joe calmly rose, put the flame on under the pot of soup, and went to the door. As he opened it, Errol fell through but Joe stepped aside so he fell not into his arms but onto the floor. His face was pale, his beard and brows covered with ice. Joe removed Errol's boots for him and said, "Come into the warm kitchen."

"I can't get up."

"Then please crawl," Joe said. "I'm sorry, but I don't have the strength to drag you."

"Where is Anna? Where are the children?"

"Where they are supposed to be. In bed asleep."

It was customary for Errol's family to be up and waiting and to throw themselves on him with joy and gratitude at his being preserved once again from nature's deadly and nonchalant embrace, often crying spasmodically from the release from fear.

Joe was not prepared to perform their part in the drama. He was not going to throw himself on Errol and wet his neck with tears. Nor would he let Errol summon his family. "Please keep your voice down so they will not be disturbed."

"They will want to know I'm all right," he said petulantly, although his tongue was thick with cold and the words came out almost incomprehensibly. He staggered to his feet, stripped off his outer garments, and tottered to the kitchen.

Joe ladled soup into a large yellow bowl and set it in front of him. "I told them you were all right and they believed me."

"But . . ."

"It doesn't mean they don't love you because they were not here weeping and wringing their hands as the hours dragged on."

"I know that."

"Good. But I would like to know that you love them equally, because it seems to me you rejoice in putting them through such hell."

"I can't help it if I get lost."

Joe sat down across from him, folded his hands, and addressed him thus: "After getting lost one time, it is given to a man to understand that he doesn't know what he is doing. Two times and he might begin to wonder why he persists in behaving like a fool. Three times and he might wonder if he is suicidal, and is bound to deprive his family of his love and support, or if not that, ask himself if he has some underlying motive for his irresponsible behavior."

"Are you judging me?"

"Yes."

"Isn't that against your credo?"

"Yes," Joe smiled. "But, happily, my credo, as you call it, is infinitely flexible. And, although a judge, I'm not a hanging judge."

"Some holy man," Errol grumbled.

"I'm not a perfect holy man. But we are talking about you and why, if you know they love you, you want to keep upsetting your family."

Errol was silent. He spooned soup.

"Do you feel threatened that Anna has come to be with me?"

"Of course not!" he protested.

"I will not be around for long and then it will be for Anna to decide what to do, whether to remain here or not."

"Shouldn't I, as the man of the family, have some say in the decision?"

Joe was thoughtful. "Not necessarily."

"We'll see about that," he muttered ominously.

Joe wondered if he had handled the situation wrongly and

decided he had, since their relationship had gone from tolerant to adversarial. Errol was scared of Anna's position as Joe's chosen one. His escapades were to assure himself of his importance to his family. Joe had been disgusted by his behavior and had acted out. He had not only judged him, he'd condemned and rebuked him—the three things a man must never do to another if he wants to live in peace.

It dawned on Joe that for the last twenty-five years he had been visited here at the hermitage only by people seeking enlightenment. Errol had come either for the ride or against his wishes, and this was Joe's first interaction with one such as he. Pilgrims spent days, weeks, months in line to see Joe for a few seconds, whereas Errol, who had waltzed in on the tails of Anna and Jacob and was privileged to live daily with Joe, didn't like it. After tonight he would like it even less, perhaps endangering Anna's own stay with Joe.

But there was no going back, no un-saying what Joe unwisely had said. There was going forward. But more importantly, there was now, the moment they were in, together in the kitchen, in the middle of the night. So Joe unfolded his hands and put his warm hand across the table and lay it on Errol's cold one.

Joe's heat penetrated Errol's body at once, brought color to his face. His down-turned mouth relaxed and the usual sparkle returned to his eyes as he raised his face to look at Joe.

9

"Do me a favor," he said, sliding his other hand over to Joe. "Cover this one, too."

Anna, sleepily, entered the room, looked wonderingly at the

two silent men who seemed to be having a séance. "Oh, darling, I thought I heard your voice. Are you all right?"

"Of course I am. Go back to sleep. I'll be along soon. You are not to worry about me. I am not a child."

Anna turned and disappeared. "Like that?" Errol asked Joe.

"Not bad," Joe said. And it wasn't bad, but it wasn't good, either. Errol had relinquished his dramatic role but wasn't giving up the role of master.

However, Joe said nothing, as he should have done to begin with, silence being truly golden. Any trouble under the sun, thought Joe, can be overcome by silence.

I should have quietly taken his hand and acknowledged his sadness without the lecturing and hectoring that went before. And yet, having spoken, I feel so good! If I had been quiet while seething inside with resentment, that would have been bad for us both. Instead, I expressed my feelings and he retorted hotly and threateningly. Now we have our moment of peace and of being our true selves.

3
CONFLICT

The monks returned to the hermitage, some coming earlier than in other years, since they were concerned about Joe and how he had survived the winter. In the fall, before they had left for their work in the world, they one and all had urged Joe to spend the winter in the town below, but he had refused.

First came Kim, the Korean marathoner, at twenty-one the youngest of the monks. A few days later from Italy came Maria, the scientist, along with the Chinese cellist, Ho. A week later, the final three arrived within hours of each other: Ed, the English poet, Helena, the African-American chef, and Henri, the lawyer from France. They were a small united nations of monks. The

South American member, Daniel, did not appear. He had succumbed to greed and envy and slunk out of sight.

After loving greetings, cheerful, welcome festivities, and long catch-up conversations into the night, there was a massive spring cleaning. The upstairs was opened up and there ensued a mighty scrubbing down and airing out of the entire hermitage. The robes were brought out of the cupboards, washed and hung out to dry on lines that were attached to iron spikes driven into the boulders. Soon the wheat-colored garments rose and fell, whirled and flapped, in the funny, puffing winds that were typical of the mountain-top spring.

They were all delighted to find Anna in residence. She was given a robe. Jacob was offered one but demurred, not feeling worthy. "Everyone is a holy person," they told him, "and these robes don't mean we're even holier, just that we're all members of this particular community. Joe doesn't want to distinguish himself. He wants us all to look alike."

"I have many more sins to wash away before I can wear this robe," said Jacob. "And that is that."

"Also," Anna explained, "he's so incredibly macho, he's afraid to look like a fool."

"That, too," said the ex–French Foreign Legionnaire. "I'm not a monk, I'm a bodyguard."

"A holy bodyguard," said Anna.

When robes were being handed out, Errol put up his hands and said, "Don't even think of it," which was all right because they hadn't thought of it. They hoped Errol would not stay for the summer. He was an ongoing irritation in their normally harmonious daily life. They were annoyed by his treatment of Anna and his general mockery of the hermitage routine, especially his flouting of the rule of silence during the day.

"He has been sent to test us," Joe said.

"We get tested by people like him all the rest of the year," they grumbled.

"Then he's just been sent to test me. So far, I'm failing the test. It's fascinating." Joe had been thinking a lot about the fact that he'd been living in such a rarefied, loving atmosphere all these years and that, were he to live in the outside world, possibly he would be quite different—a cantankerous, difficult person.

He had always diminished his holy-man-hood to himself as well as to others, but now he wondered if he'd underplayed it half enough. He talked it over with Ho. "I think if I were not on this mountain it might turn out that I was not a holy man after all," he said.

Ho simply laughed and walked away.

The children wanted robes, and they also wanted shaved heads. When it was Anna's turn to have her head shaved, she said she didn't want to. Unfortunately this became a bone of contention with the others. They felt she was setting herself apart from the rest of them. Or they felt she was too attached to her prettiness. Or, worst-case scenario, she was not shaving her hair because Errol didn't want her to.

There was a lot of lively discussion around this issue. Everyone voiced an opinion. Joe heard them out. Anna did not assume a defensive stance, listened eagerly to all that was said, but still did not want to shave her head. In her mind, she said to herself that she would hang on to her hair unless Joe saw fit to hand down a decree against it.

She certainly did not want to cause dissension. She didn't want to be different from the others, not at all: she was proud to be one of them. She looked into her heart to see if it was vanity at work, but she did not feel that it was. She had never thought of herself as a beauty, quite the contrary. She'd been scrawny and homely as a child and kept that image of herself into adulthood. She had never used makeup and, in her life as a mother and nurse, had always dressed in a practical, colorless fashion. She had gone through a brief passage of sowing wild oats during which she had been unduly attached to a pair of cowboy boots and a leather jacket with long fringes on the sleeves, but that wonderful period had been curtailed by pregnancy and marriage. She still had the cowboy boots, had actually worn them on her first pilgrimage to the hermitage, and had brought them with her this time, too. She felt she stood tall in her splendid boots and that in them she had an extra bounce to her step.

As for her hair, except that it was red, it was nothing special, neither short nor long, curly nor straight. She knew that some women had a fetish about hair. She didn't. Nor was this a Samson issue. She did not feel she'd be deprived of her strength by shorn hair. It was just a part of her that she felt belonged. She was surprised there was all this fuss about it, that meetings were being called, and that everyone had so much to say.

"I actually like having my hair off," said Kim. "It seems to make me lighter for my running and feels a lot cooler, too. But I can see it might be harder for a woman."

"It's not harder," said Maria. "It's easier. Nothing to bother about, no combing or styling. Hair is a hassle."

"I have to admit, I never liked my hair," said Helena. "I pretty much wear it this way all year round now. And, of course, as a chef, there is nothing I hate more than hair getting in food."

"Musicians are supposed to be long-hairs," Ho the cellist said. "I felt much more romantic and dashing, playing with my long hair all aquiver, an extension of the notes. And the dramatic forward flop of it as I made my bow was incredibly pleasing. But I gave it up for the good of the group."

"Maybe also for the good of your cello-playing," said Ed wryly. "However, it is essential for poets to have long hair. Who ever heard of a bald-pated poet? If we are going to start patting ourselves on the back for shaving our heads, I am surely the noblest."

"Lawyers' hair should be just so," said Henri. "But not just so shaved." He laughed. "Nevertheless, my friends, I bet you have noticed that, unlike losing a limb, it grows back."

"You see, Anna." They turned to her. "It grows back. You are making too much of a big deal out of it."

Anna finally spoke. "It is all of you who are making a big deal out of it, not me. I simply don't think it's important."

This silenced them and they were thoughtful for a few seconds. Before they could come up with rebuttals, Joe said, "I agree. Shaving heads is not important. And not shaving heads is not important."

4
A PRESENT

Joe, the children, and Anna were sitting on the ground, on the edge of the slope, watching the sun go down, which they declared as good as television, the way the clouds changed color and shape. Also, instead of fifteen inches, the screen was without end.

Jimmy said to Joe, "Today I was fighting with Melissa. Mom, as usual, told me to be nice, but why? Sometimes I don't feel like being nice. Sometimes being nice is boring."

"That's when you should just go off and be by yourself," said Anna, "until you feel nice again. Not take it out on other people, especially someone smaller than you."

"I just want a reason to be nice," said Jimmy. "Then, when I feel mean, I could think of the reason and stop."

"Good idea," said Joe. "Anna, give Jimmy and Melissa a reason."

Anna thought for a while, then said tentatively, "Being nice is good luck."

Joe laughed. "I like that. Why didn't I come up with that in all these years? Children, your mother is truly a wise woman."

"But what is good luck?" Jimmy asked.

"Maybe it's getting presents," Melissa said hopefully.

"I used to feel very lucky to get a present," Joe said, "until one time some years ago. It was when the hermitage was just beginning to be discovered by people. I lived here with four monks and we were very poor. It had been years since we had bought any new clothes and we were a very ragtag band of holy men. One day, a woman who had enjoyed a fruitful visit with me said she wanted to give us some money. I accepted it with thanks.

"Only a month went by and back she came wanting to know how I had spent the money. The five of us stood in a line displaying our beautiful robes, which were more of a reddish brown color then.

"'I am pleased,' she said. 'I will go away satisfied that you are wearing my robes.'

"'Not really your robes,' said I, 'for you must remember that some one grew the cotton, another picked it, another spun the thread for someone to weave the cloth, which yet another person dyed. And then, after we bought the cloth, Jorge, here, cut the pattern, and John sewed the cloth. So the robes are a gift from many hands.'

"'That is just nitpicking,' she said. 'Let me take a picture so I can show my friends that the holy man and his monks are wearing my robes.'

"'Absolutely not. That is forbidden.'

"She laughed and danced away and snapped the shot. By then we had turned away or thrown up our hands, but I suppose she captured the robes. Maybe not, though. I have never heard of a picture stolen of any of us that came out.

"Well, children, this woman became an incredible pest. She always wanted special treatment when she came and she came often. Because we were wearing what she insisted on calling her robes, she felt she owned us.

"I have to confess to a nasty thrill the summer she came and found us in brand-new costumes, the beautiful wheat-colored robes that we wear to this day.

"Her face clenched in a terrible frown. 'What happened to my robes?' she asked furiously.

"'They have become wonderful cloths which we use for dusting and scrubbing,' I said, showing her the cut-out squares, which were thin and frayed but still useful.

"'You can have your old rags,' she said.

"'Thank you so much,' I said. 'At long last your generous gift belongs to us.'"

5
THE PICTURE

I s it true," Anna asked, "that pictures of you and the monks don't come out?"

"Yes. Once there was a young photographer down in the town who got the idea he would sell pictures of the holy man to people who were on their way up the mountain to get in the line. He felt sure that in no time he would be a rich man. He had heard that the holy man himself took turns coming to town to get supplies, so he thought he would be able to take my picture furtively. There was one problem. No one knew which of us was the holy man, since we all dressed the same.

"That isn't strictly true because for all the years I've been here, I've always gone to the park to play with the children and, although different monks have come and gone over the years, only one old monk has remained year in year out to play with the children, many of whom are now grown-ups, so really the whole town knows who I am at some level of their consciousness.

"Anyhow, this photographer sneaked around and took photographs of each one of us and figured afterwards he would find out which one was me, even if he had to climb the mountain himself to look at my face. But, when he developed them, they were out of focus or overexposed or underexposed or the monk's face was turned away or someone had got in front of him just before he shot the picture. He decided he should quit before the word got out that he was a terrible photographer. He had gone from wanting to make a fortune to just not wanting to lose his business.

"But many of the townspeople, the grown-up children I had played with, when they learned what he had tried to do, stopped coming to his shop. You see, the town is very proud of the fact that it has never tried to commercialize the presence of the holy man on its mountain. They are pleased with all the extra business the pilgrims bring and are content with that.

"I was curious, so I went to the young man's shop. Alim was his name. I told him I would like to buy the pictures. I recognized him from years ago. He had been a very nice little boy. I guess he recognized me, too, because after I left he hung up a big sign saying, THE HOLY MAN SHOPS HERE." Joe laughed. "The man was incorrigible."

Jimmy said, "But, Joe, there should be a picture of you for when you die."

"Do you think so? Then why don't you draw a picture of me?"

"Okay."

"Me, too," said Melissa. "I want to draw one, too."

The sun had set and it was dark by now, so they went inside and established themselves at the long dining table with paper, pencils, and crayons. Joe sat still, posing for his picture. Jimmy got lost in an elaborate picture of dinosaurs. Melissa, however, stuck to her guns and soon presented Joe with a picture of himself. His head was oddly shaped with extra large ears, different-sized eyes, a potato nose, and open mouth slightly smiling. His arms grew out of his head and his legs came out of his chin—with spidery hands and feet. He appeared to be flying.

Joe was so happy. "This will be my official portrait," he said, "for when I die."

6
AMBITION

After the children had been put to bed, Anna found Joe in the common room talking with the others, and when there was a pause asked him, "What happened to the photographer, Alim, when he put the sign in the window saying the holy man shops here?"

"Well, a week or so went by, and then he arrived on my doorstep, huffing and puffing and very red of face. In those days the line was short and spent itself each day so, unless I was busy around the hermitage, a visitor got an audience fairly soon. I remember that I was slightly busy in that I was whittling some chopsticks and amusing myself by carving little animals at the top of them." Joe broke off his tale and asked the monks wonderingly, "Whatever became of all those chopsticks I used to whittle?"

They all looked guilty. Maria said, "I think every monk who's spent time here with you has a pair of those chopsticks in his home. I know I do."

Joe laughed. "Then I better make some for Anna. Anyhow, back to Alim. We sat outside in the boulder garden or, rather, I sat and he stood. The birds were busy feeding their chicks, and I remember also that there was a predatory bird circling above, endlessly patient, waiting for its moment to swoop down for one of the babies, periodically casting its sky-crossing shadow on the nests. One of us always tried to be in the nesting area during that vulnerable time, but still, nestlings were lost, drops of blood scarred the rocks.

"Alim began talking at once and never drew breath. He must have been breathing through his ears. He said, 'Just because I have been imaginative enough to put that sign in my window, they want to run me out of town. The holy man shops everywhere, they say, and the rest of us do not have signs. So? Is it my fault that they never thought of it? Is it my fault that in this town no businessman has had an innovative thought for a thousand years? Correction, in fifteen years, the years that you have been here and dampened the town's ardor for progress. I want to get ahead, make a fortune, make a name for myself, but they just care about making enough to eat and drink and having time to watch the game of the dappled ponies.'

"Ah ha, I thought, my wild young Alim has been to war, has

drawn blood like our sky circler is trying to do. You see, Anna, as Ho can tell you, or Jacob, only men who have been in combat are able to see the game that is played from the backs of the stumpy-legged ponies."

"Or so the old warriors say," Maria whispered to Anna.

Joe continued. "Alim, who had run up the mountain in the heat of his wrath and the sore sense of being terribly wronged, went on to say, 'It is probably because you played with us as children that we all wanted to grow up and be like you.'

"'Remember, Alim, how we used to all sit together and breathe?' I said. 'I think you have forgotten how to breathe. You might take a moment now to inhale and exhale, to relax. Won't you please sit down?'

"'No, no, I can't stay,' he said, waving his arms as if my inhales and exhales were swarming around his head. 'I just thought you should know that you are wrecking my career.'

"'I think it is fine you are such a hard worker and that you want to excel at what you do. I am a great believer in that. Probably you have a family to support and need a lot of money.'

"'No,' he said, pacing about, 'I don't want to saddle myself with a family until I put some money aside. My store is the first photography store this town ever had. I have to travel far and at great expense to buy cameras and film. It is thanks to me people have family pictures to hang on their walls, have pictures to go in the newspaper to show what has happened each week. I have worked hard, fifteen hours a day, to get ahead. Now everyone is up in arms because I tried to take your picture. Why wouldn't they, too, want a picture of you if they love you so much? Answer me that.'

"He managed to stop for a minute, to stand still and look down at me where I was sitting. I said, 'I like to think of myself not so much as a person but an idea. I think that is what the townspeople like to think, too. I am like the mountain itself, a thing that is there, enhancing the town, a thing to feel good about. They would not need a picture of the mountain on their walls since it is so built into their consciousness from birth, just as it doesn't occur to one to record in a picture the tree that stands outside one's window.'

"Alim didn't seem to be listening to me. Instead he looked at me, looked all around us, and then looked up at the sky as if he'd only just arrived—not only at the hermitage but on earth itself.

"'Do you know, Joe,' he said slowly and rather awkwardly, 'I have never before been this far up the mountain. It is . . . so nice.' He took a deep breath and then, with the exhale, much to his surprise, came tears. They poured from his eyes. You never saw such tears."

Joe fell silent.

"Then what happened?" Anna asked.

"I'll tell you what happened. Young Alim stayed on the mountain for two and a half years. Then he went back to town and got married. His business is thriving, although probably he would be a little richer if he didn't have so many children and if he didn't so often go to watch the game of the dappled ponies."

7

A NEW ORDER

Before the great long line of the pilgrims would start to arrive, the monks wanted to build a small courtyard at the front of the hermitage where Joe could sit to receive people.

Previously he always greeted the pilgrims standing at the front door. "Yes?" he would say, and they, thinking him an old servant, showing no deference, or even much friendliness, would say, "I want to see the holy man." Not hello, how are you today, may I please come in?

Joe would wheel around, saying, "Come with me," and whisk

them along through the hermitage in record time until they arrived at the back door where he let them out and said goodbye.

"But I have come to see the holy man," they would object, and then Joe would say, "You have already seen me." Most times he added, "If you will treat every one you meet as a holy person, you will be happy."

And that would be that—which, they'd realize later, was a lot.

Of course there would be some people, more enlightened ones, who would recognize the holy man in Joe and greet him courteously. He would ask them to sit down on a bench just inside the door and they would talk together.

Now Joe was too weak for all this to-ing and fro-ing through the hermitage and thought that he would just sit by the door to greet the pilgrims, and the monks could take turns ushering them through and out the back, giving them the word. Toward that end, they were building a walled-in area, with a bit of shade where he could sit outside during the receiving hours. Kim, that great wrestler of rocks, was fitting stones together without cement to make a bench for Joe to sit on.

Kim was being careful not to disturb any of the rocks where the birds were nesting. He moved with T'ai-Chi slowness as he wandered and pondered through the mountain's boulder garden, eyeing the different shapes and sizes.

28 If there were times that his artist's soul played with the idea of carefully moving a nest to another venue so that he could have a stone his heart was set on, a stone that seemed created just

for a certain spot in the body of the future bench, he fought the desire, knowing it would blight the bench to do so and that somewhere on the mountain a better rock was waiting, gloriously nestless.

Jacob and Errol hired a string of the mysterious ponies that were pastured halfway down the mountain and took them to the western foothills, a dry grassy area where, along the side of a certain stream, was ideal clay for the making of adobe bricks. They bagged it and ponied it and hauled it back to the hermitage where, when mixed with the dry winter grasses and hermitage spring water, bricks were formed of it, then put in the sun to dry. These would form the courtyard walls. Errol, using his architectural skills, had designed the walls to integrate handsomely with the fine plain style of the hermitage.

Anna worked alongside the others with a happy heart and, since her hair was always getting in her eyes because of the wind, ended by, no, not shaving it after all, but trimming it shorter. She cut up a dress to make a kerchief to wrap around her head, and one by one the others asked for a kerchief, too, so in the end, or at the beginning as it might have been, they were alike after all in wheat-colored robes and gaily printed kerchiefs. The children wore them, too, and even the bodyguard felt he was worthy of the kerchief.

Joe, feeling pleased, thought, Perhaps it is a new order of monks. Yes, the monks of the holy kerchief. The monks of Anna's holy kerchief. The holy Annakerchiefians.

8
POISON

Errol had been busy getting the clay for the adobe and making the bricks and supervising the building of the courtyard, so he'd been in fairly good spirits. As the project reached conclusion, he began to grow restless again. One day he asked Anna to take a walk with him so they could talk without being overheard by the monks and children. Anna suspected that he wanted to get far enough away to yell at her in private.

When they were several hundred yards along the Back Trail, he began fitfully, "I don't understand what we're doing here. Enough is enough." Anna walked faster, picking her way with sure steps, so he had to scramble after her. "For years you told me you were having dreams about a holy man somewhere in the world. You began to look for him and, last summer, you came here and you found him, and it actually seemed that he was waiting for you. But you didn't stay, you came back home." Anna listened but still hurried along so as to be out of sound and sight of the hermitage.

"The next thing that happens is Jacob arrives in Dublin from out of the blue, having tracked you down. He says the holy man is sick and alone and needs you. So off we all go. That's fine. It's an adventure for me, and I know it's important to you. I figure you'll nurse him back to health and then we'll go home. Why am I getting the feeling that we're never going to leave this place?"

By now they were a good half mile from the hermitage on a round knoll overlooking the valley and town which, today, was covered by a low-lying fog, which made Anna feel they were much higher in the world than the three thousand feet of the mountain—on some Himalayan height above the clouds. "Errol, I'm glad you brought this up because I've been meaning to tell you that Joe and I are going off together for a week."

Errol frowned and said sarcastically, "How long exactly have you been meaning to tell me this?"

She smiled. "Just for a couple of days."

"And where are the two of you going?"

"I'm not sure exactly, but, you see, his teacher is very sick, maybe dying. Joe feels he must go to his side. He hasn't seen him for more than twenty-five years, but he spent ten years of his life with him and they are very close. Let's see, Joe was on in his thirties when he found this teacher, in Cambodia, but the teacher was only twenty. So now he must be only fifty-five or so."

"I don't like this one bit."

"It is something Joe feels he has to do. He wants me to come along so as to continue his teaching. It will be a learning journey for me."

"It is dangerous for an old man and a woman to travel alone in this part of the world."

"I think we'll be taking planes and trains. The only tricky part will be getting Joe down the mountain, but we can get one of the ponies for him to ride."

"I will go with you."

"No, Joe wants just the two of us to go. And you'll need to care for the children."

"I'll be damned if I'll do that. It's one thing for you to drag us all here. Now you intend to go your merry way without us."

"It is only for one little week. Just think of it as a business trip like the many ones you took from Dublin."

"Listen here, Anna, I am the man of the family . . ."

So he began and worked himself up into a great anger, feeling ill-used by his wife, ill-respected, feeling he was losing control of the marriage and that Anna was being too free with herself. He said unkind and even abusive things to her, but she remained calm. Anna was a person without anger. She felt sorry for Errol, that he had so much anger inside him. She wished that this story could end like the story of Alim, that Errol would quit his outburst, take a deep breath and release his tears. Then he would stay on the mountain and learn to live happily ever after.

At the same time she understood his frustration. He missed the city, his work, his friends, the pubs, the football matches. He missed coming home to a waiting wife with dinner on the stove, where he was lord and master instead of sitting down each night at a communal table of silent monks. However, she remembered well that he'd had just as much anger in him in their Dublin life as he had now, maybe more.

Anger, greed, and ignorance were the three poisons, Joe said. But how did one treat such a poison? What was the antidote to anger?

"Say something," he yelled. "Why do you just sit there?"

Sometime during the tirade, Anna had sat down on a rock. "Being nice is good luck," she said, feeling a little silly, feeling this would not necessarily do the trick as it did with the children.

"Being married to you is bad luck," he said. "Because you are so nice you just make me feel like a jerk."

There was a long pause and then he said, miraculously, "And you're right. I am being a jerk. Go ahead, take your holy business trip. I'll watch the kids. And then, when you come back, we'll take it from there."

33

Anna looked in his eyes, hoping to see them clear and loving, but she saw anger there still, anger in his heart, in the tenseness of his shoulders, and in the veins that stood out on his neck and throbbed with his heightened pulse. She had the feeling that his being nice by saying what he had just said was not good luck, that this was one of those bad presents like Joe had received from the robe woman.

9
AN IDEA

 $\mathbf{M}$ y teacher, Chen, is very sick," Joe announced to the monks that night in the common room. "Tomorrow I set out on a journey to go to his side. This is important for me. You may not feel I am up to the journey, but I assure you I am. Anna will accompany me. I know some of you will wish you were also invited along, and I am sorry not to include you. It will be a necessary learning journey for Anna. Jacob and Errol are not here just now because they have gone for two of the ponies to take us down the mountain in the morning. In this age of jet travel, I anticipate that the journey and visit will take only a week. If any pilgrims arrive while I am gone, I would hope you might start receiving them yourselves, taking turns as the holy man, which all of you are. Or else I would elect Kim to be the door greeter. He's so young that the pilgrims will not think that he is the one they have come so far to see and we can continue to play our awakening trick on them to help set their feet on the path."

Joe continued to speak in his gentle voice, which was still audible over the whispers that were building to a low-grade hubbub. "Forgive me if I seem brusque. I know you want to discuss all this until the cows come home, but it is an accomplished thing."

The vocal din subsided to a murmur that was still insistent and which Joe still ignored.

"Perhaps you feel we are deceiving the pilgrims not to tell them I am away, but I think not. It is in the line itself that their trip becomes worthwhile, opening the door to the wisdom that is already inside them. Remember that what separates me from other holy men is that I am not a man so much as an idea.

"By now, all of you have got that idea, although perhaps one wouldn't know it now with this continuous susurrous of grumbles."

Ed, the poet, raised his voice. "You are not an idea. You are a man, and you are the man the pilgrims come to see, not us."

"Yes," agreed Maria. "We are all holy persons, but you are the holy man. We can't deceive the pilgrims. It's not right."

Joe looked surprised. "I honestly do not believe I am any holier than you. Lately I have thought I am a good deal less holy. It is you who can take your holiness into the daily struggle, survive and thrive, while I just sit here."

"We carry your wisdom and compassion out into the world. We are the mules, the holy mules, but you are the holy man," said Henri.

"Very well. But let's not deny the pilgrims the glorious walk up the mountain and the chance to talk with you."

"I think we had better put a sign at the beginning of the trail, saying that the holy man is gone," said Ho. "That is the fair thing."

There was a murmur of sorrowful agreement.

"Indeed you are mules, stubborn as mules. Already it looks like I'm no longer the boss around here. Very well, the holy man is gone, but not yet. For my farewell, tonight, I want you to talk about what has made you exceptional in your field. This is for Anna. You have become successful, even famous, through talent, discipline, and perseverance, the three main qualities for achievement. As well, you chose to set off on the journey toward wisdom and compassion. What is the extra quality that has made you such consummate artists in your work? What has made you unique? Helena, please go first."

10
GENEROSITY

Helena stood up. Her brown skin glowed in the soft evening light. She cupped her chin in her hand. "Well, now, let's see. Hummm. I've got to think a little about this, Joe. I know the notion first came to me to be a chef when I was little and heard a story about a king who wanted to eat something that was very hot and very cold at the same time. Chefs from all around the land tried to satisfy his fantasy, and no one could do it. I think it was a kitchen boy with a wide-open beginner's mind who took the necessary intuitive leap. He set to work and came up with the very first hot-fudge sundae.

"So I got interested in cooking and every time I ate something good, whether cooked by friends of my mom's or some restaurant chef, I tried to get the recipe, and wouldn't you know, no one would ever give it to me, at least not the whole thing. Great cooks are the most withholding darn people you ever knew. They want to be famous for whatever their dish is, and they figure if they give it away they give away their hard-won celebrity, too.

"I vowed that when I got famous I was going to tell everyone how to cook just as good as me, and that's what I'm doing. Instead of being a big deal chef in a famous restaurant, I've got all my cooking schools. And another thing is, I cook food that's good for you. It doesn't just taste delicious, it makes you healthy and glad. I grew up to believe French cuisine was the greatest but, man, it is so full of fat and sugar, it's not funny.

"You know, you go into the projects, and other places where poor people live, and no one knows how to cook anymore. They go to McDonald's or get take-out. It's hamburgers and pizza for these folks, if it's anything. It would break your heart to see how those little kids never come home to a nice home-cooked dinner, the good smells, the family closeness of sitting around a table set pretty with maybe a flower or two in a vase in the middle. That's something they just don't have any experience of. So I try to teach the mothers and fathers how to shop, prepare, and present healthy food. It doesn't even cost them more than all the take-out and Big Macs. I go into their area, open a little restaurant to show them what I have in mind, and then I start giving classes.

"So, what am I trying to say here? For that matter, I think I forgot exactly what it was Joe asked!"

"You've answered it, Helena," Joe said. "You're a unique chef because of your generosity."

11
CHANCE-GIVER

I'll go next," said Henri, standing up to speak in lawyerly fashion, "since Helena's talk segues into mine." His bright eyes flickered around the room, and even in the flowing wheat-colored robe he managed to look like a sharp dresser.

"A lot of those little kids that don't get to eat healthy food at the family kitchen table grow up to be the scum-of-the-earth. They grow up stupid, mean-hearted, greedy, and angry. You might say they are brain dead and soul dead. All they care about is money, and when they get it they haven't an idea in the world what to do with it to make their lives better. They think a new pair of sport shoes will make everything cool, then a leather jacket, and a new car if they live that long. But it doesn't make everything cool. They still don't have a home with good food and some flowers on the table, nice music, and loving companions.

"In Marseille, there is a lot of rage among the young who are Algerian or Moroccan, sometimes Vietnamese or Chinese. Education is available, but they drop out too soon. There is so much unemployment, they feel they have no future and, of course, there is racism. For them, there is only the solace of heroin, and the community of gangs.

"If they live, they come into the justice system, but there's no way in the world they're going to get a good lawyer who will care about their case. Until they meet me. Why do I care? Why do I want to get these monsters off free so as to send them back onto the streets to steal some more, perhaps to kill? Because I am their chance. Not their second chance, their first. These kids who never once had a chance, now, by some miracle, have me. They get my expertise as a lawyer and my friendship as a man. I tell them I'll get them off and get them help, and if they do get straight I'll help them to stay in school, maybe even see them through university, if they can hack it. Meanwhile, my young protégés can come to my apartment any time they want and have a home-cooked meal cooked by my in-house chef, trained by Helena. They can bring the flowers for the table as long as they don't steal them out of someone's garden on the way. It's quite a sight seeing these hard cases come up my steps carrying a bouquet of posies. But that's nothing. Now, some of them are growing flowers!

"I'm a great lawyer because I believe that everyone deserves a chance at redemption, a chance to begin again and do it right, and I'm here to give them the chance. All that scum-of-the-earth, after all, is holy-scum-of-the-earth."

"Henri's unique gift is the same as Helena's," Joe said. "Generosity. The more you give, the more you get back. Generosity is inexhaustible."

Henri added, "By the way, my success rate is pathetic, about ten percent, but you can believe they are all going to be First-Chance-Givers, too, helping others out of the mire. The ripple effect is going to take some hundreds of years, but it's rippling right now as I speak."

He reached up to his throat where, normally, he would straighten his tie, but there was no tie. He smiled and sat down.

12
FAILURE

I owe my success as a scientist to failure," Maria said. She was short and plump with flashing eyes. "That is something you don't hear so much about: all the times you try something and it doesn't work. I'm talking hundreds of times. All the experiments that go belly-up. It can get you down. But that's when you try again. All that trying and failing, that's what makes you good. And that's the fun of it, too. What a bore it would be if everything worked out fine the first time you tried it. How would you grow? How would you learn? People tend to give up after a lot of failure or rejection. I believe you have to embrace failure, really love it, say, oh thank you, this is great, now I get to try again and do it right, or at least do it better, come a little closer to what I was after, to what I was trying to find out." Her intense eyes unfocussed, looking back.

"There was the time, which is how I got famous, that I didn't find out what I was looking for, but I discovered something else along the way, something no one else had found or understood before. Eureka! Wasn't it lucky I hadn't let myself get too discouraged to go on?"

She smiled and sat down, saying, "I guess that's it. Short and sweet."

Joe said, "Maria thinks she's talking about failure, but she's really talking about perseverance. It is a sublime quality, a noble virtue. Without perseverance, there can be no greatness. But failure is its instigator. When you do something good, it is tempting to stop right there and hold on to it for all you're worth. But that is just playing it safe. Let the victory go. Give it away. And take in the failure instead. As Maria said, embrace failure, it's come to help you grow. Thanks, Maria. Ed, how about a contribution from you?"

13
LAZINESS

I was always a slob," Ed said. His lanky body sprawled lower in the chair as if to emphasize his point. "Never was there a man who loved sleep so much as I. I only got up in the morning because I knew that pretty soon I could lie down again and read a book, muse about things, or take a nap. I was the kind of child of whom they said, 'He lives in another world.'

"I decided early on that being a poet was the life for me. It would require the least exertion.

"As an adult, I discovered that there was always a woman who was more than happy to take care of me, to cook and clean, keep a roof over my head and clothes on my back, in return for which she got to tell people she was The Poet's Girlfriend. Sometimes years would go by before she realized that this was not a good deal, before she realized that it *was* a deal, it wasn't love.

"I was a taker. When I began to spend summers with Joe and live with a group, none of whom was my girlfriend, I had to change my ways. I had to exert myself for the good of the group, and I found it a joyful experience. I felt happier, more energetic, and more disciplined. I wasn't in another world; I was being attentive to this world, to my every action. When I went home, I began to live alone and take care of myself. I am still lazy. I still lie around a lot and do nothing, and my flat is messy. The refrigerator is a horror, and we won't even talk about the grease in the stove. Someday it will go up like a torch.

"I wander in the woods hours on end, not even really thinking. But my creativity seems to lie in my laziness, and as long as I am not hurting others with it, or taking from others because of it, then I am okay and my poetry is okay, too."

Joe commented, "You could say instead that yours is a gentle life, an uncontrolled life. You allow for the unpredictable, the spontaneous. Because you are so incredibly relaxed, you are open to experience and thought. You allow space in your daily life for your art to enter. All this sounds better than laziness, doesn't it? But you are right, it is all laziness."

"I am trying to learn from Ed," Henri said. "I am so controlled, efficient, and industrious. There's nothing I fear more than a day with the calendar empty. Two days and I would shoot myself. I am in love with my schedule, the busier the better. I haven't done a spontaneous thing since the day I was born."

"You came here," Joe said.

"It wasn't spontaneous. It was on my list of things to do in the future, and one day the future came. Even so, I only have you down for three weeks this spring. It's pitiful. My only three weeks in the year to let down. And I use up one of them just going through telephone withdrawal."

Helena said, "Just keep on smelling the flowers the killer kids bring you. You'll be okay."

Joe said, "Both laziness and overaction spring from fear of life, death, of being who you are, of knowing who you are. They are escapes. However, both action and nonaction can be creative ways to live if you pay attention and if you spend time with yourself, being yourself. Then you will know the truth that is in you and the holy person that you are."

Joe invited Kim to speak.

14
ONE WITH
THE UNIVERSE

Kim, as he talked, owned the room. Moving around, his every motion and gesture was a joy to behold, so natural was it, understated, efficient, graceful, and uncontrived. "I was born with many gifts," he said. "The bones and musculature, the size and shape, to be a precision runner. I sought out the best coaches and threw myself into my training with all my heart. I had all the gear with which to excel, but it wasn't enough for me. I wanted nothing less than to be one with the universe, to link up to the energy, the breath of the universe, and therefore enable myself to go farther and faster than was humanly possible.

"This sounds ambitious, but it actually meant giving up

ambition, giving up my ego. That's when I found Joe for a teacher so that I could learn to give myself over, learn to relax my body and have my mind be still even as I ran at phenomenal speed for hours. I learned to spurn the physical self. Running, I am no longer muscles, organs, bones—my molecular structure becomes one with the very air itself. I am as light and free-moving as air. I am no longer human. Except"—Kim laughed—"at such a moment when I trip and fall. Then I become strangely human again, so human that I bleed abundantly and sometimes, I'm sorry to say, cry tears of the same abundance. So, perhaps I haven't quite got it down perfectly. I must still be clinging to my ego, which trips one up every time. I haven't completely blended with the breath of the universe. But that's my aim.

"As for a name for this quality, I'm not sure. Any ideas? And, please, don't say stupidity."

"Fearlessness," Joe said. "We will call it fearlessness. To seek to do the impossible, to give yourself over, mind, body, heart, and soul, to air, which is to dare to be nothing. Fearlessness is not bravery, is not courage. What is it? It is calmness."

Errol and Jacob, having returned to the hermitage with the ponies and tethered them by the spring near bursting clumps of new spring grass, had entered the room at the beginning of Kim's talk. Joe explained to them, "We are each taking turns telling of the special quality within ourselves that has contributed to our achievement and perhaps made us unique. Ho, I guess you are the last to speak."

15
AROUSING
COMPASSION

There is a quote by Congreve: 'music has charms to soothe a savage breast.' When I was young I heard someone misquote it, saying that music can soothe the savage beast. It captured my imagination and set me on my cello-playing path. When I became a performing musician, I never got to play to the wild tigers and lions I had imagined as a child, but I knew that in my audience would be men and women who were savage—who were cold and uncaring, selfish, angry, consumed by ongoing desires to possess rather than to give. What was wonderful was that such people came to hear music. They liked it. In the sheath of steel over their heart was a tiny crack to let in soothing sound and allow rapture. That meant there was hope for them. If there was a crack, the crack could widen. If I played really beautifully, if I was full of the music, if my music was informed with the glorious idea of love and laughter, then, unbeknownst to the beast, the crack would widen and their heart would be touched. When their heart was touched, the idea of compassion could be awakened within them and they would begin to begin to change—for the good."

Ho fell quiet and the others remained still. After a while, Joe made a summation. "From Helena and Henri we have learned the precept of generosity, from Maria the virtue of perseverance. Ed has shown us the creative power of an uncontrolled life, Kim the freedom of fearlessness, and Ho tells us that the mastery of an instrument played with all one's soul can melt the stoniest heart."

Then, unexpectedly, Jacob spoke. As always, it was with an effort, as if the words were being wrung from him. "I guess everyone here knows that I joined the Foreign Legion when I was a youth not to soothe the wild beast but to be one. I deludedly thought it would be a grand adventure, but it was a slaughter. Three years later when I came home, not a hero but a killer, I built that steel sheath over my heart, thinking to protect myself. I put the war behind me and vowed to tell no one about it but to try to live a decent life. I did so. I studied and worked hard. I was successful and good to my employees. I married, had children, served my town, gave to the poor.

"But I hadn't changed. I was only a secret-keeper, a pretender. I hadn't even begun to *begin* to change because there was no crack in my careful armor. The boy slaughterer was imprisoned. He was in mortal shame, begging to be let out and forgiven, not forgotten. It was not until my forties that my armor began to crack, but not for the good. I began to disintegrate as a person. Each crack was like a wound. I was depressed, alcoholic, caught in my ego, angry, and hateful. But something awakening must have got into one of the cracks. Maybe at someone's home I heard one of Ho's recordings, maybe one day on television I saw Kim win a marathon and heard his transforming words or, on my travels, stepped into one of Helena's restaurants and felt an imminence of peace. Whatever it was, I got it in my mind to come to Joe for help and to dare to present not my pretend self but the boy slaughterer himself.

"So this is not to tell you what to be, it's what not to do and be. Don't keep secrets. Don't pretend. Don't be a hypocrite. Don't manipulate others. Don't be dishonest." He sighed heavily. "That's it."

Joe then inquired of Errol if he would like to say something.

"No, no thanks. I'm afraid I just don't get it. Sometimes I think you're all living in another world up here."

"Anna?" Joe asked, letting Errol's words go by.

16
ANNA'S SECRET

Hearing Jacob talk about the harm of keeping a secret, I'm going to tell you what I've never told a soul except, recently, Joe.

"I guess Jacob and I are changing the tenor of the evening. Instead of describing what makes us good, we are explaining why we are bad. But I'm glad to speak to charitable ears, because it has been a terrible burden. Like Jacob, I have been a pretender."

Anna got up from her chair and stood before them, a small, slender woman who radiated such a joy of life that one felt good just looking at her. The faces watching her and listening grew more composed, wore involuntary smiles.

"I'm a nurse. And I'm not a very good one, really, since I can't abide blood. It makes me faint and nauseous. And I always feel an underlying anxiety that I'll do something wrong. I hate to give shots or hook up an IV. My mind tends to wander. I worry about parceling out the different medicines, fearing an error. I often take exception to the doctor's choice of treatment. It's all a nightmare, really. It's hell on earth."

There was some laughter and Anna was surprised. She flushed, laughed a little herself, and continued. "Then why am I a nurse? Well, you see . . ." Anna stopped, cleared her throat. "One day when I was a little girl a friend of mine was sick and couldn't play. I sneaked into her bedroom through the window to see what was the matter. She was lying there sleeping, looking pretty ghastly and, well, I did seem to see what was the matter. It was in her stomach. So I put my hands on her tummy and went into sort of a dream and the next thing I knew my friend was hugging me and saying, 'Oh Anna, I'm so glad you're here. Let's play.'"

Now the monks looked at each other with raised brows. Errol's brows grew tight and close.

"That was when I first identified my gift and that is why I became a nurse, so I could be a healer without people knowing I could heal. They would just think I was a really good nurse, which I'm not. But, you see, I didn't want a lot of fuss. I wanted to just be me. I think Joe just wanted to be Joe, too, but look what happened. I mean, he is still Joe, that's what's so great about him. But I couldn't have handled people knowing I was a healer and coming to see me by the thousands. I wanted a normal life—if there is any such thing.

"Then I kept having the dream about Joe, and looking for him. When I finally found him, and when Jacob brought me back to him, I think that it wasn't because I was his chosen one. It was because I was meant to be with him at this time of his life, and meant to learn from him so as to know what to do with my own life and gift."

Anna breathed deeply and smiled. "So, the truth is out. I feel better. All these years everyone has thought I was such an amazingly great nurse and I wasn't at all. I was only a healer."

Anna was astonished when everyone burst out laughing and one by one came to give her a hug and a kiss. Except Errol, who said to Jacob, "Everyone here is stark raving mad and now Anna's gone crazy, too."

17
DREAMS

Outside, the night sky was cloudy. A halo surrounded the nearly full moon. Kim said, "Joe, today I finished this bench for you. Will you sit on it with me now?"

Joe sat down. "This is a fine bench, Kim. The stones still seem to contain the heat of the day, the beams of the sun, nice on my old bones. It is so comfortable. How did you happen to find such very soft stones?" Joe teased, "Probably you changed their molecular structure."

Kim looked abashed. "Yeah, I guess I went a little too far in my talk, a little over the top."

"I admire people who go too far."

"Joe"—Kim hung his head, hiding his face—"I feel like you won't be coming back to us, that this is goodbye."

"Anything is possible, Kim. We can all be taken at any minute."

"I have learned the lesson of impermanence. I have come to grips with my own death. Why is it I cannot bear the thought of losing you? The idea of your no longer being here on this earth is intolerable. It fills me with the most crushing pain."

"It is the hardest thing in life to lose our loved ones. There is no greater sorrow, Kim. I know how you feel. Not a day goes by that I don't think of my wife and daughter and feel my throat close up. It was fifty years ago, that car crash."

"What was she like, your wife?"

"She was very serious. I loved to make her laugh." There was a long pause. A cloud covered the moon, the air darkened, and their surroundings retreated. Even the hermitage became form-less. Their robes were a smudge of light and their locked eyes were clear and bright.

"She and my little girl live on in my heart," Joe continued, "and all these years I have often visited them in my dreams, vis-its that seem as real as life. She has never once mentioned what an old man I have become. It doesn't seem to matter to her." Joe put his arm around Kim. "I am an old man, I've fulfilled my years. The real pain of loss is when the person is young."

"Do you think, when you die, you'll be with your wife and child again?"

Joe shook his head. "No, I don't."

"Will you still have your dreams of being with them?"

Joe smiled. "What a wonderful idea." Joe kissed him. "If I do, I will hope to have many dreams of being with you as well."

18
GOODBYE

One by one the monks came and kissed Joe good night, but when Ho came it was, like Kim, to say goodbye. "Well, old friend, old warrior, I guess this is goodbye for now."

Joe stood up and embraced him. "Noble Ho. Soother of wild beasts. What a wonderful last night this has been with you all."

"Good journey, Joe."

"It will be a fine journey, an important journey. I go to save my old teacher."

"Is that why you are bringing Anna? To heal him?"

"No. I am bringing Anna simply because I want her with me at the last. Ho, look after Kim, will you? This will be a hard time for him."

"Of course I will. But who will look after me?"

19
LEAVING THE
HERMITAGE

Early the next morning, Anna and Joe mounted the dappled ponies, which Joe called the stumpy-legged ponies. They had short, strong legs built for mountain trails, but they were also agile and fleet because of the polo-like game they played when ridden by the ghosts of warriors past. Their coats, spotted with varying shades of bay and gray, were beginning to shed their winter thickness. There were no saddles or bridles, so both Joe and Anna hiked up their robes and straddled the ponies' bare backs. They twined their fingers in their shaggy manes. When Anna mounted her pony, everyone smiled to see that she was wearing cowboy boots. This was indeed a quirky wise woman.

Jacob would walk along with them so as to return the ponies to the pasture afterward.

Anna had already made her farewells to Errol and the children in the privacy of their room. Although enchanted by the idea of the journey with Joe, she found it a wrench to leave Jimmy and Melissa and her heart was unquiet about Errol.

Her family and the monks were out to wave them off. It was silent period, so no one spoke. Kim stood back, away from the others, afraid of making an emotional display. He had a secret plan to run down the Back Trail in order to, so to speak, cut them off at the pass, where the Hermitage Trail met the Back Trail. In this way he could have a last look at Joe.

But Ho, charged to look after Kim, intuited his plan—not hard to do as Kim was wearing running shorts and shoes. Ho had his own plan to stop him and set him to work white-washing the new courtyard with him and the children. He knew that if Kim were allowed to run after Joe to the trail crossing, then he'd decide to run on to town and then probably run after the car to the airport. Too heartbreaking. Ho's plan was to keep Kim here and work him until he dropped, until they both dropped. So now he drifted back and stood nearby, ready to grab him, ready if necessary to wrestle him to the ground.

Joe put his hands together in prayer position and held them

before his breast. He bowed to his monks, his face calm. They returned his bow. Then, in the blink of an eye, he was trotting away.

Joe wanted to stop and turn for one last look before his pony took the hairpin curve, for he knew he'd never see the hermitage or his friends again, but he felt embarrassed to do so. He did not want to seem to milk his leave-taking. The pony was going so fast. If he was going to look back, it was now or never.

It flashed through his mind, his coming to the mountain a quarter century ago when he was almost fifty. He found the right site, camped out at first, then gradually put together the bits and pieces to make a hut which, in time, and with help, became the first sturdy room of the hermitage, adobe built on a rock foundation, what was the common room of to-day. He flashed on all the different monks who had been with him over the years, the building of more rooms, the coming of the first pilgrims and then the ever-lengthening line. All this passed through his mind as the curve was rushing toward him that would take away his last view. Why did he need another look? It was engraved in his mind's eye, from camping site to full-blown hermitage.

As it happened, the pony made her own decision, for these stumpy-legged ponies were showboaters who exulted in fancy footwork. They were given to spontaneous dodges, darts, and pirouettes, and this one did a sudden two-hoofed whirl before taking that first curve, and so Joe got his look: the sturdy white building, the rocks and birds, the string of monks looking after him, Errol and the little children waving, Kim and Ho in a cloud of dust as they wrestled together on the ground.

20
LIVING TRUTH

Down the mountain they went, keeping their silence, Anna first, then Joe, followed on foot by Jacob, descending the jagged trail which Joe had walked a thousand times. He wished he could have walked it this last time, but it was out of the question. He barely had the strength to hang on to the pony's mane. But never mind. He enjoyed every moment of the ride: the wonderful vistas, the masterful strokes of white against the blue canvas of sky, with a spray of birds or a lone bird wheeling and turning in the air like the ponies did on the earth. The attendant sound of water was the promise of earth's renewal for another year.

Their ponies whinnied to the herd as they passed the pasture.

Joe thought of all the times he'd sat on the fence and watched The Game and was tempted to do so now, but the ponies weren't playing, they were munching grass. "Goodbye ponies," he said softly, and he knew many of the neighs and whinnies were for him as well as his mount, saying: "Goodbye, holy man."

Then they entered the woods, through the trees of clattering leaves, along the rushing creek, treading on the thickly growing trillium and iris. Out on the low foothills on the verge of the town, their eyes and noses were ravished by the spring lilac, bushes as big as trees: purple, lavender, and white. They passed under long arches of the scented clusters, then soon the ponies' hooves were beating on the cobbled streets.

Now Joe took the lead and soon stopped at a pleasant shop near the center of town. "This is the photography store of the famous Alim," Joe told Anna. "I have a secret errand to do here, and on your return I want you to come to this shop. Alim will have something for you. Will you remember?"

"Your memory is better than mine, Joe. You will remember."

Joe said to her somewhat firmly, "It is time to begin thinking that I will not be with you when you return."

"Yes, you will," Anna said just as firmly. Joe laughed.

Jacob, who had caught up to them by the time Joe exited the shop, said, "Joe, I want to go with you and Anna. I will keep out of your way, but I feel that both of you need my protection. The world is not like it was when you were last abroad, Joe. Hunger and drugs have stained men's minds. Human life means nothing to these people. You won't have a chance. It is my purpose in life, now, to look after you and Anna. That is what I live to do."

"It can't be done, Jacob. We must look after ourselves as best we can because we must have autonomy, which is freedom. If we put ourselves in the hands of another, no matter how loving, we would be imprisoned. Friends must look out for each other, depend on each other, but not protect each other. If we were protected, we would not be attentive or mindful, therefore only half alive. Finally, needless to say, I would be embarrassed to have a bodyguard, and thereby seem to value my life so highly."

"But the world is evil, Joe."

"No, Jacob. The world is good. People are holy, every last one of them. That is my belief and therefore it must be my attitude. If I traveled with a bodyguard, I would be a living lie."

21
THE
COLLECTOR

Jacob said goodbye to Anna and Joe and then, forlornly, went off with the ponies. Joe walked the few steps to the park to play with the children, and Anna separated from him to pick up the plane tickets and to find a taxi to the airport.

It was market day and farmers had come with their produce to sell in the open air of the town square. Old cars vied with horses and donkeys and even with oxen which pulled rickety overladen carts. Sometimes a new model automobile meandered through, looking like a futurist fantasy against the medieval background, moving silently amidst the riotous other vehicles. Anna knew that in cities where such cars were the norm, people were more aloof. There was rarely this relaxed, friendly atmosphere with people calling back and forth to one another, passing the time of day, laughing, haggling, drinking coffee out of minuscule cups, or quaffing the 180-proof locally distilled product which, luckily, was served in minuscule containers as well.

The piles of fruit and vegetables elated her eyes. Even the flowers paled beside them. Anna thought there must be something special in the soil to produce such intensely colored carrots, beets, and broccoli. Even the celery was stunningly green and the humble mushroom a brilliant brown. Anna chose from the fresh loaves of bread and mounds of cheeses for their luncheon, also purchasing a small bag of tomatoes. There was no restaurant in the airport. It was more like a bus stop than an aerodrome, its one or two planes a day coming and going on some secret schedule of their own.

After her errands, since she had a passion for coffee and there was none at the hermitage, she allowed herself one of the small cups. It fulfilled her desire and satisfied her high coffee standard—black, mud-thick, and sugary, delivering a tremendous jolt.

The town seemed to offer just one taxi. Although old, it was clean, with the muffler system intact. The driver, however, was a sorry excuse for a man, all skin and bones and rags. She directed him to the park, smiling kindly at him, but got no answering flicker, only a look of jaded weariness as if she were asking him to carry her on his back instead of in the cab.

Joe was waiting at the park entrance, which, strangely, was

marked by two stone elephants, the beast being no native to this land. Joe was surrounded by children, all of whom looked solemn. Anna thought that, seeing how frail he was today, they must guess they would never play with him again. But just as she formed this thought, they all burst out laughing. Joe turned away from them and got into the cab.

"Always leave them laughing," Joe said.

"But how did you do that? They were all looking so sad a minute ago."

"I wiggled my ears and crossed my eyes at the same time. Very hard to do. Takes years of practice. I urge you to learn the trick and carry on the tradition. Although I don't believe I've ever known a woman who could wiggle her ears. It must be a recessive male gene or part of the Y chromosome."

"We'll see about that," Anna vowed.

The driver, who hadn't started the taxi and was obviously listening, turned around and astonished Anna by wiggling his ears. Joe laughed. "I think I remember you. Could it be Ezla?"

Ezla grinned and Anna saw he was much younger than he had first appeared. "Joe, I am so happy to see you."

"Please talk English so Anna can understand. I remember you were a smart boy. I'm sure you've learned many languages."

"That is true," Ezla continued in English. "All these years I have waited for the day you would step into my cab, but it was a hopeless hope since you never have the occasion to go anywhere."

"Well, I do today. To the airport, please."

"First, may I ask your helpful advice?"

"Surely. In one moment." Joe turned to Anna. "Before I forget, Anna, all the children want kerchiefs. Will you see to it upon your return?"

"Yes, Joe," Anna said sadly, suddenly feeling there was no point in saying they could both see to it, because such a scenario had become a "hopeless hope," so certain did Joe seem to feel he would not return, almost bent on it. But why, then, was he going away? Why did he not want to die at his beloved hermitage with all his friends?

"Ezla, please tell me your trouble," Joe said encouragingly. He and Anna listened to the taxi driver's story.

"At the turn of the century, in this town, there was a potter named Blackie, called so because he was darker than the rest of us. He lived simply, making his pots and selling them to the people. They were strong and serviceable in practical shapes, and no one much noticed how beautiful they were until, many years after his death, some foreigners came looking for them. Almost every family had them but, of course, many had broken or cracked over the years. Those that weren't damaged were sold to the collectors for what seemed like attractive prices at the time.

"By the time I was grown up enough to appreciate Blackie's pots, there weren't many left. I decided to buy the ones that were still in the town so as to retain Blackie's heritage and, that accomplished, began to look farther afield for them. I would work hard, pinch pennies, then take off on a hunting trip for Blackie's pots. This took me out in the world, and I had many adventures. Because of this pot search, my life was full, or so it seemed. Gradually my search changed from joyful to grim. His pots were in every corner of my house, but did I ever look at them, use them, or enjoy them? No, no, and no. Some of them never came out of the box they were buried in at the time of the purchase.

"In fact, my mission to protect his pots and return them to his homeland has changed to one of depriving the world of their usefulness and beauty. My house is a crypt. But I can't stop. Meanwhile, I go around in rags, pretty much as you see me now, and no woman will look at me. If they do look at me, they soon find I will bore them to death, since all I talk about is Blackie's pots, much as I am doing now. Pots, pots, pots.

"I would be a rich man if I sold them off, but I am completely unable to part with even the most paltry. The least I could do is turn my home into a Blackie museum so people can come and see the pots but no, no, and no. I am paralyzed with fear that someone will take one of them from me. Joe, this is not a fun life. Help me."

"Hummm," Joe mused. "You must know everything there is to know about pot-making by now."

"Of course."

"About the clay and the firing and the different glazing techniques?"

"Yes, I am certainly an expert."

"That's good. Because my theory about obsessive collecting is that it is repressed creativity. My advice to you is to make a pot yourself."

"What an extraordinary idea." Ezla's haggard face lit up. His eyes seemed to come forward from their skull-retreat.

"Now, my friend, you must not expect it to be a very good pot, but if you make another, and another, and so on, then one day you might find you hold in your hands a rather nice one. Even if you don't, I promise you will have fun trying. You will feel an excitement when you bring your own handmade pot out of the fire that is quite unlike any feeling you got from buying one of Blackie's."

"Thank you. I already feel the first stirrings of my future creative fervor. You have changed my life. You are right, this is what I am meant to do. And you, the holy man, our Joe, have given me permission to begin. I will take you to the airport and, please, the ride is on me."

During the ride, Anna said, "Joe, I love the answer you gave Ezla. You are so wise. I would never be able to come up with such a response. I feel like such an idiot, really."

"No, no, and no, as our friend Ezla would say. You are a wise woman. It took me all my life to learn the little I know and can impart, but you, as was my teacher, Chen, are a natural. You have a loving innocent heart and a lucid mind. You are not supposed to be me. Only remain you in all your Anna-ness. You may lose yourself sometimes. You may lose your gift for healing, too. But you can come back, better than ever. Remember that pain is often thrust upon us in this life, but suffering is voluntary. Don't suffer, Anna, keep your happy heart and you will always be able to help others."

Anna was quiet for a while, then asked curiously, "Do you have any of Blackie's pots at the hermitage?"

"Why, yes, the oval-shaped vase that we put flowers in, with the strange gray glaze."

"I know the one. It is beautiful. And yet, it is quiet. A modest pot. You can tell, as a potter, he never looked for fame and glory, only made pots as a part of his day, like eating, drinking, and sleeping, like going for a walk."

When they got to the airport, and were out of the cab, Ezla got out, too, and said, "I heard you mention you had a pot of Blackie's up at the hermitage. His gray glazes are particularly hard to come by. Tell me, Joe, please, I beg of you, what will you take for it?"

22
HELPING

At the airport, Anna saw three beggar women sitting together. One was blind, one had no arms, one had shrivelled legs and sat in a cart.

"Can we do anything for those poor women?" Anna asked Joe.

"No. But they can do something for us. Come on."

Joe and Anna went over to the threesome. Joe greeted them in English and they responded in kind.

"Can we show you around?" the blind woman asked.

"Can I carry your luggage?" asked the armless one.

"Run any errands for you?" asked the woman with crippled legs.

Joe gave money to the blind woman, whose fingers delicately passed over the notes as if she could determine the denomination thereby. "We want to have some kerchiefs made up for the children in the park like the ones Anna and I are wearing. Go to the cloth store," he told the blind woman, "and pick out the prettiest material."

He turned to the armless one. "Cut the material into squares this size. We will want about twenty of them." Joe took off his kerchief and showed the size.

To the shrivelled-legged woman, he said, "Run the squares of cloth over to the seamstress's shop and have her hem them for us. For these purposes, use the money I have given you and please keep the change."

"Very good," they all agreed. "We will have them here for you at the airport upon your return."

Joe and Anna left them to check in for their flight. "So, you see," Joe said, "they are not beggars. They are a corporation. Three individuals united in one body. They are a constant reminder to me not to try to do (or be) everything myself, to admit there are some things I cannot do and for which I must ask others for help.

"Because, when you ask someone for help, you give them a chance to help. You make them feel worthy. These three women would be helpless without each other, but together they are as sound as you or me.

"They survive not by being helped by each other but by helping each other. Then, having formed the corporation, they make a living by helping others."

"I am terrible at asking for help," Anna admitted.

"Because you are in a helping profession and a helper at heart. Would you please carry my bag over to that bench? It is getting too heavy for me."

"Sure," Anna said, taking up the shabby old carpet bag that probably contained one more robe and his toilet articles and a book of poetry.

When they were seated, Anna thought for a while, then took a bundle from her pack along with her Swiss Army knife. "I bought some food for us while you were at the park. Um . . . would you please prepare a lunch for us?"

"Happily," said the holy man. "Very good, Anna," he added.

23
THIEF

Anna and Joe were at the airport two hours before the small propeller plane landed on the field. While waiting, they sat silently on a bench, ate the bread, tomatoes, and cheese, then rested.

Anna worried that the flight might be a shock to Joe's system after twenty-five years at the hermitage, but he was calm and meditative the whole three hours, even during a rough patch at twilight time when the plane bucketed through the air like a wild horse being broken.

The plane landed at a much larger airport in a different land. They headed for the toilets, which were in rooms next to each other. Anna gave Joe his carpet bag. While in the woman's room,

Anna carefully put hers and Joe's passports in the purse she wore around her neck under her robe. It also contained her plastic bank card and some cash. She carried her pack on her back. She decided to tie her kerchief around her neck to compliment her boots—a sort of cowboy theme.

When she exited the room, Joe was waiting for her but had been confronted by a man with a knife to whom he was passing over his carpet bag. Anna was furious to think that this scum-of-the-earth would attack one who appeared nothing more than a small, old, ailing monk who had taken the vows of poverty.

"Joe, what's happening?"

"Please, Anna, don't make a fuss or you will upset this poor man. He wants us to give him all that we own. He is quite desperate."

"He doesn't look at all desperate. He looks like a rat to me."

"I understand English," he said in a thick accent, glaring at Anna, waving his knife in front of her face.

"Anna, he must be a desperate man to fall so low as to take from others. His family needs food, no doubt. Perhaps his wife is ill."

"Joe, there are thieves everywhere these days. He probably wants to buy drugs. What kind of a person would steal from a holy man? A low-down, dirty, scum-of-the-earth-rat, that's who."

"My wife is very sick," he said.

"Oh, sure," she said scornfully.

79

Anna placed her small body in front of Joe. "If you touch the holy man, your knife will have to go through me first."

"No, Anna," Joe insisted. "We must help him out. Give him your pack."

Anna, ignoring Joe, looked around. "Where's the security in this place?"

Joe took the pack from Anna's back and passed it to the thief, but he was unable to receive it since the hand that didn't hold the knife already held the carpet bag.

"Wait, there is more," Joe promised him. "Anna, your boots are very valuable, are they not? Such beautiful hand-tooled calf-skin. Am I right in describing them as calfskin?"

At the first mention of boots, Anna had bent her knees so that the robe covered them up. "Well," Joe said sorrowfully to the thief. "Anna is deeply attached to her boots. But I have a real treasure for you. Look!"

He slipped a locket from over his head. "It is silver." He opened it up and showed it to the man who now stood with his hands at his sides, the knife drooping from one hand, the carpet bag slipping from the other, the pack at his feet. "Look closely, it contains two curls." The thief peered into the locket. "One is from the head of my wife, the other from my child. The two curls are looped together. The color is as vibrant today as the day they were killed."

"Joe, you are not to give this vile person your dearest trea-sure." Tears poured forth from Anna's eyes. She sat down on the concrete floor and began pulling off her boots. "He shall have my boots and all the rest of our things and that is enough."

"Yes, yes, please take Anna's wonderful boots, but have the locket, too. Anna, what else can we give him?"

By now the thief, his face a mask of bewilderment, was backing away. "I don't want the locket. Or the boots. I don't want any of your stuff. Here!" He kicked the shabby carpet bag over and threw the pack on top. What do you think I am? Get out of here! You are some kind of crazy people. Stop giving me stuff."

He turned and fled.

The holy man smiled at Anna and helped her up off the floor. She felt very embarrassed about the boot business, the way she had bent her knees to cover them with her robe, an involuntary action which she knew Joe had not missed. Again she wondered how for even one minute he could consider her a wise woman. Yet, to her amazement, Joe, by virtue of his outrageous kindliness, had put the thief to rout.

He put his arms around her and kissed her. Her body was trembling from the aftershock of the encounter. "Anna," he said, "my dearest Anna, how very brave you were."

24
THWARTING
BASENESS

Their next flight wasn't until morning, so Joe, who seemed to speak every language, arranged for a taxi to take them to a nearby hotel.

It was now night, dark and cold. Their room was small but clean with two single beds. They weren't hungry, having eaten all the bread, cheese, and tomatoes as well as some food they'd been given on the plane, but Anna said she would like a cup of coffee.

"The first floor of the hotel seems to be a sort of cafe. I'll go down there."

"I will go with you," Joe said.

"You must be dreadfully tired."

"Never mind."

Joe led the way to the cafe, which was next to their hotel, not a part of it. He secured a table near the door, far from the jukebox which released hectic jangling sounds. The floor was beautifully tiled, but the paint was peeling on the walls and bare bulbs illuminated the room. It was cold and bleak. A miasma of smoke hung over the bar where the customers had congregated. This was not a tourist hangout.

When the waiter didn't come to their table, Anna went to the bar and asked for coffee. Ten or twelve swarthy men were clustered there, all of whom stopped talking and drinking to look at Anna. She was the only woman in the cafe and she was the only pale white person and certainly the only red-haired person.

She began to think this was a bad idea but returned to the table with the coffee. She untied the kerchief from her neck and tied it around her hair, which in her mind seemed to blaze redder and redder, like a beacon.

The men were still looking at her and seemed to be edging over to their table. She gulped the coffee.

Joe was sitting in his usual placid way, looking out the window, but she knew he had eyes in the back of his head. "This is a mistake" she said quietly. "I don't think women go into bars in this town. At least not this bar. Let's go back to our room."

Joe stood up, but by now the men had formed almost a complete circle around their table. "You come with us," they said to

Anna. Three of the men had taken rocks from their pockets and were knocking the rocks together in a united beat. *Chunk, chunk, chunk.* It was a terrifying sound. If they'd pulled out guns and shot them into the air it would not have been as scary to hear as this monotonous chunking sound. Anna yearned for the holy bodyguard.

Joe was holding a gold coin between his thumb and forefinger and he set it on the table for a tip. The men took their eyes off Anna and watched the coin. Another coin appeared between his fingers, then another. Each time, Joe set it on the table until soon there was a small pile of gold with a nimbus of light around it. The men were mesmerized. They only had eyes for the money. Suddenly, Joe scooped the pile up in both hands and threw it into the air. All the men put out their hands trying to catch it. Their rocks dropped to the floor, and soon the men dropped, too, on their hands and knees, looking for the coins that had fallen.

Joe and Anna darted out the door and into the hotel, swiftly climbing the stairs to their room. Once inside, with the door locked, Anna sat down on her bed and Joe lay down on his, both of them panting.

"Joe, where did all that money come from? You seemed to pluck it out of thin air."

"I did. It was an illusion."

"But I saw it."

"There was no money."

"Golly!"

"Yes, I had to distract them. Such a shame that I had to appeal to their baser instincts, but there really wasn't time to appeal to their inner holiness. When individual men become a mob, their holiness almost entirely disappears. I had to make do on the spur of the moment. Sad to say, there is nothing on earth so distracting as money. It works every time."

"It was brilliant. I suppose I should learn that trick, too, in order to be a first-class wise woman."

Joe smiled.

"Maybe I can learn to wiggle my ears, cross my eyes, and perform illusions all at the same time."

"I doubt it, Anna. But after I have rested I will teach you the trick. You need a real coin to begin with. All the others are from the power of the first coin's suggestion. That and hypnotism."

"But I saw it, too."

"Mass hypnotism."

"Do you think they are still looking for the coins?"

Joe laughed. "By now they are looking for me. Happily they have totally forgotten about you."

"Joe, I'm sorry I went for the coffee. You knew it was a bad idea but instead of stopping me, you simply came along. Why?"

"I knew you wanted a coffee, and I thought you deserved to have one."

"Well, it was thoughtless of me and I'm sorry."

25
LOVE

Joe was asleep. Anna washed up and put on her nightie. She picked up a chair that was in the corner and carried it over to Joe's bed. She sat and looked at the holy man sleeping peacefully. She felt honored to be with him while he slept. She went into a healing trance and looked for the sickness in him, but she couldn't find it. He is hiding it from me, she thought. She held out her hands and ran them over his entire body about a quarter inch from his skin, not touching him but letting her healing energy enter him. She did this over and over until her arms were tired. Still she sat, watching over him in his sleep, loving him with all her heart.

She didn't remember getting into bed, but when she awoke some time in the predawn hour she was under the covers. Joe was sitting in the lotus position on the floor, meditating, and she noticed that the chair had mysteriously turned in the night and was now overlooking her bed, not his.

26
BLAME

The next day was spent in the airport and on a jet plane. Once again Joe took it all in stride, sitting calmly as if he were on his chair at home or on one of the boulders in the garden. Anna enjoyed it all, watching the people in the airport, striking up conversations with some of them, gazing out the plane window, or at the in-flight movie. Joe enjoyed her enjoyment.

Nothing momentous happened until, having arrived at their destination, they got a taxi to their hotel in the town. Joe was pointing out sights to Anna and she was eagerly looking and listening when suddenly, crash! Their taxi hit another car.

Anna and Joe tumbled together and slammed against the

front seat but were unharmed. The driver was definitely un-harmed since he leapt furiously from the cab as if catapulted. So did the other driver so that their bodies practically collided in the street alongside their blended vehicles. Much shouting and gesticulating transpired. The words rolled from their tongues, Anna thought, like waves from the sea, and although they were probably saying very unkind things about each other's mothers as well as each other, the vocals were magnificent in their timbre and range. Each man, in his rage, seemed to be trying to take flight. Their driver jumped up and down with both feet off the ground, and the other driver whirled his arms through the air with his body on a strong forward tilt.

Words failed to bring about any solution and knives were drawn, but by then Joe had opened his door, stepped from the cab a bit shakily, and gone over to the furious twosome. He barely opened his mouth. He could not have said more than two or three words when the men were swept by a miraculous calm.

Anna was astonished. Where a second ago steam had been coming from their cars and fire from their mouths, where long daggers had been glittering in the sun, now two placid men stood as gentle as lambs, listening as Joe said a few more words. The next thing Anna knew, the men were shaking hands, exchanging cards, and Joe and the driver were back in the car. The two drivers were able to disengage the cars and soon Joe and Anna were mov- 89
ing on to their destination.

"What on earth did you say to them?"

"I will tell you when we have checked into our hotel," Joe said.

In due course they were established in another small but clean little room and Joe told her the story. "Naturally each driver was mightily blaming the other and each seemed to have ample proof of the other's bad driving record, ongoing illegal maneuvering, and renowned bad character, including unacceptable sexual practices.

"I simply told them it was my fault. I went on to explain that I'd been pointing out the window at the time, which probably had distracted my driver and confused the other driver, who perhaps interpreted it as a turn signal. They were both extremely happy to accept this explanation.

"You see, Anna, one thing that people hate more than anything is to take the blame. Every cell in their body revolts. Even if they *are* to blame, they can't take it. They will deny it with every atom of their being and come to believe within seconds that they are the blameless one, ill-used by all the others.

"The truth is, taking the blame, even if you didn't do it, smooths the knottiest situation spectacularly and immediately. Everyone feels better. The wrong-doer retreats from his defensive posture. The blameless person or persons get to be proved right, which is highly gratifying. It even allows for productive conversation about it."

Anna pondered. "But what about the poor person who has taken the blame and must suffer accordingly, perhaps even be punished?"

"Strangely enough, he gets to be admired. Perhaps not right away but eventually. He is certainly appreciated for solving the problem and bringing tranquility to where uproar prevailed. He will be treated with surprising leniency."

Anna looked dubious.

"Just like last night. You were quick to take the blame for the ugly situation in the cafe, which wasn't in the least your fault but which I considered great of you to say. Blame-takers are generally admired because it is considered such a devilishly difficult thing to do. A person would rather expire than say they were wrong. Both those men were prepared to die over not being in the wrong about that extremely minor accident where so little was at stake."

"But I have known some people," Anna said, "well, one woman anyhow, who is every minute saying how sorry she is and how it's all her fault and apologizing right and left until people want to slap her face and pull her hair and set her clothes on fire."

"That is different. That is a woman with a self-esteem problem or a woman who secretly enjoys the feeling of control she gets for driving you all crazy. That is not the same as the person who is courageous enough to take the blame in a time of trouble. The blame-taker is a happy person."

27
THE WHINER

For dinner, Joe and Anna went outside to buy food from the stalls that were set up along the harbor. The choices were many and the different dishes were hot, spicy, and tasty. They sat on a bench taking pleasure in the mild evening air and salt-borne breeze, after the long stuffy hours of travel in stale air.

Joe had been whittling Anna a pair of chop sticks, and he presented them to her now. At the top of each stick was a tiny rabbit, one on all fours, one standing on his back legs, intricately carved. Anna was charmed.

After they had eaten (Anna using her new sticks), they sat silently for a while as was their habit. Then Anna said, "I am still wondering about this blame-taking business and why the blame-taker is a happy man."

"Well, let's look at his opposite, the whiner. The whiner blames everyone for everything. Whatever is wrong in his life, be it his health, job, family, friends, or finances, he finds someone to blame. He is always in a predicament, and it is always someone else's fault. You would think that his incredible ability to spread the blame everywhere rather than taking it on himself would make him a happy person, but he is never happy."

"Perhaps we are talking about taking responsibility."

"No, not really. Because our whiner will often take responsibility for anything good that happens. Then he will take all of the credit and say it is due to his craft, wile, intelligence, or hard work. Whereas our friend the blame-taker, when something good happens, will say how lucky he is or that God is so good to him. Our happy blame-taker can experience gratitude. Gratitude is second nature to him. As a result, he lives in a state of grace that is brought on by his happy positive attitude.

"He always expects the best. His friends, made nervous by his buoyant attitude, say, 'Aren't you setting yourself up for disappointment? You are in for a big fall.' But he isn't, because when the disappointment comes, although he feels it, and suffers, he is quick to take the blame on himself. He says, 'Oh, that was my fault, I didn't do such and such or should have done thus and so.' And then he lets it go and thinks what a beautiful morning it is or, 'Gee, this tea tastes good.'

"Yet the whiner never lets go of a disappointment. He milks it for all it's worth, even years later."

"I think I understand," Anna said,

Joe laughed. "You certainly ought to, since I'm describing you. You are a happy blame-taker."

"Do you think so?"

"Evidently."

"For sure I'm happy. My life is so wonderful it seems like magic. I am blessed with good luck."

Joe laughed again. "You see, it is exactly as I have expounded. You take the blame but not the credit."

"I hope all this doesn't make me a Goody Two-shoes."

"Don't worry. You are too committed a boot-wearer for that. You are the airport warrior."

28
LOVE

Joe and Anna sat quietly and watched the lights come on in the boats and in the houses on the hills across the water. The water reflected the lights in wavering lines and dappled distortions. An apricot moon appeared from behind the hills, astonishing them with its size and hue. Stars appeared, pricking through the gathering darkness as if pushed from the other side. Street lights were lit and beamed down on their bench. As one, they stood to go, but then Joe tottered, reached for Anna, and shakily reclaimed his seat. He was pale, almost translucent. Fumbling, he took a pill from his robe pocket and brought it to his face. He seemed to grope for his mouth, then, missing, dropped the pill. Anna, fearfully attentive, caught it and put it between his lips.

In a little while, Joe was breathing normally, and his pulse was restored to its slow and steady beat. His color was still bad, but it was hard to tell with the yellow street lamp.

Anna asked him if the pain had been very bad, and he admitted it had. She wanted to take Joe to a hospital for observation over the night, but he refused. She begged him, but it was useless.

"Tomorrow I'll be at my teacher's and then all will be well. I think if we walk slowly and you let me lean on you a little, we can make it to our room. Thankfully our room is on the ground floor tonight and thankfully we don't have to run to it, pursued by a mob of angry men."

Anna thought last night seemed long ago. Every hour, every minute with Joe was so abundant, the journey had assumed the size of a large part of her life.

Later, as Joe slept, Anna again sat in a chair and gave Joe healing energy. It was not good enough. So she got into bed with him and held him in her arms throughout the night.

29
THE
TEACHER

The next morning, when Anna woke up, Joe was in sitting meditation, lotus position, and she was relieved to see how well he appeared to be. His color was fine. She could feel his energy. She went down the hall to shower, and when she returned Joe was moving about. "Today will be a wonderful day," he said.

While they sat on a bench waiting for the train that would take them to his teacher, Anna asked Joe to tell her about him.

"Chen is a genius," Joe said. "Although Chinese, he grew up in a monastery in Cambodia, and by the time he was sixteen, which was when I met him, he was already enlightened. But that was not enough for him. He had a vast hunger for knowledge. When he was almost twenty, he went to study at Oxford and asked me to come with him. Even though I was long ago graduated from a university, I obliged. After four years of study, he wanted to travel the world, seeking out wise men, talking with them. The capacity of his mind was inexhaustible and his physical health, strength, and energy were phenomenal. Finally, I could no longer keep up with him and his insatiable curiosity, and so we had a parting of the ways. That's when I went off alone and found my hermitage. I haven't seen him since."

"It must have been hard to part after so many years."

"It was. But he had already attracted a large following. It was no longer just the two of us. We were taking different paths. The time had come. Still, he will always be my teacher and I honor him as such."

"And now he is sick?"

"Yes. The world must not lose a man of such gifts. I believe he is one in the line of prophets, such as Christ and Buddha, Lao-tzu and Confucius."

"Religions were founded in the name of those prophets, but if it is Chen's aim to do so, I can see why you two separated, because you have always wanted to send people on their own way, trusting in their holiness within, not draw them to you as followers."

Sensing a certain disgruntlement in Anna, Joe said, "You

need not dislike Chen's way in order to appreciate mine. In order to discover the truth, we must have no preference, no opinions for or against. Opinions are the prey of the open mind. Only be serene, Anna, and you will see the truth."

Anna knew she was discriminating like crazy. For some reason she had closed her mind against Chen. "I'll try," she said, blushing.

"Although you may see and hear some unexpected things today, accept them with a good spirit. A helpful position will be to maintain silence. Stop talking and, if possible, stop thinking."

In a short time, Anna had to put Joe's injunction to use, for on the train they sat with a young woman who, it soon transpired, was going to study with The Teacher. Joe's teacher, Anna learned, had become The Teacher, and he had his own Universe-city.

Anna's eyes grew wider and wider as she listened. To matriculate at The Teacher's Universe-city cost as much as any good private university for the first four years, but then, after learning The Teacher's system, one stayed on for free, working in a communal way. One never left. It was a complete commitment. However, he didn't accept just anyone. One had to be young, healthy, smart, and talented. He had his own system for living and learning, which involved art, music, and dancing as well as work and study, proper eating, exercise, and rest. Sex was allowed but no marriage or children.

The more the young woman talked, the more carried away she became, perhaps due to the receptiveness of her silent listeners but more likely, thought Anna, because of an underlying nervousness about what lay ahead for her.

"Those living at Universe-city will never die. Nobody ever has. Nobody even gets sick."

At this preposterous statement, words burst from Anna involuntarily. "Of course nobody has died yet, since he only allows in the young and healthy!"

"No, you misunderstand. The only reason he wants us young is so that our minds will be open to the experiment. Also, he doesn't want people who have spent dissatisfied lives going from one guru to another."

Joe explained to Anna, "Chen believes it is possible to learn how to live in the fourth dimension here on earth—the fourth dimension being time. By fine-tuning the mental, physical, emotional, and sensory, this dimension can become available to us— just as Kim tries to achieve with his running—being breath. We all have had some small experience of standing outside of time, of being one with the universe. My teacher believes that it can be developed into being the norm, the significant everyday existence instead of the rare, illusive, momentary epiphany. Once abiding in that dimension, one would be out of reach of death."

"Yes, yes, that's it," said the young woman. "But how do you know?"

"Why, I was his first student," said Joe, smiling.

Anna looked glumly out the window where it had begun to rain. She did not like the sound of any of this. It sounded elitist as well as preposterous, like developing a superrace only without the breeding.

But Joe had warned her she would hear unexpected things. She must go along with an open mind and a happy heart. Not talking. Not thinking.

She tried to erase the frown that had gathered on her brow, forcing a smile to her lips and placidity to her forehead. Sometimes a forced smile worked as well as a real one, fooled you into feeling better. Joe, looking at her reflection in the rain-swept window, seemed to nod approval of her forced facial rearrangement, her fake serenity.

She began to feel better. She let her thoughts go with the passing landscape, leaving some in the trees, some on the sloping ground, some in the occasional ponds. She released them all, even the ones she was most attached to, that she would like to explore, like the idea that Chen was a snake-oil salesman. She witnessed the jumble of her thoughts coming into her head and being jettisoned. Go, she told each new arrival. Jump off the train. Goodbye.

Her mind became empty and now on her lips was a gentle smile—a real one.

30
TRICKSTER

There was a high wall around The Universe-city and, at the imposing gate, a gate house. In the gate house were guards who refused Anna and Joe admittance, their name not being on the list of those expected that day. Their garrulous train acquaintance was allowed through, given a guide who, Anna surmised, probably whisked her off to a thorough physical, then put her in a holding pen until the test results came through.

Joe asked if he could send his name in to The Teacher and was told he was out for a drive. "In that case we will wait here for him. Is this the only entrance?"

Told that it was, he and Anna settled themselves to wait. In the following hours no one else came except three trucks full of young people who had been laboring in the fields and now were through for the day.

All about them was agricultural land, bordered by hills and, to the far west, a mountain range. The rain had let up and the air was fine and fresh. The sky was lowering, giving a crystalline clarity to the landscape in the way that bright sun only confuses. "It seems the rain showers have drenched my eyes along with the land, wiping the slate clean for a new way of seeing," Joe said. "What a masterpiece this world is! I feel the sight of it burning into my soul, branding me with an earth iron, so that if I should chance to go to another planet, the aliens will know at once where it is I come from just by looking into my eyes. They will see green fields, purple mountain ranges, blue skies, sunset clouds, the everlastingly rolling radiant seas—and be stunned."

"The whole idea of a brand is to return you to your rightful owner," Anna said.

"I am my owner," Joe smiled.

They sat on the ground, leaning against the towering wall. Anna conjured up images of her husband and children and tried to beam loving thoughts to them. She did this often during each day since the hermitage was without a phone and she was completely cut off from them. I love you. I will be home soon. I'm having fun with Joe and will have stories to tell you.

She felt as though her thoughts were being received, maybe by Jimmy, and Jimmy would tell Errol and Melissa.

At last the sound of a powerful motor heralded The Teacher's coming. A dot on the road soon became a long, low, gleaming, silver sports car. Two other cars followed.

The gate was opening for the automobile's nonstop entrance, but Joe planted himself in front of the oncoming car. This automatically ejected the guards from the gate house and, with a screeching of brakes, two men jumped from one of the following cars. Seeing the burly men and their scowling faces, Anna couldn't help but reflect on what Joe had said to Jacob about having a bodyguard, and her mind was hardened more against Chen.

All four of the brutes were prepared to seize upon the old man in the wheat-colored robe, with the gaily printed kerchief fluttering on his head, but The Teacher cried, "Stop!" as he exited his own car and waved aside the guards. He enfolded Joe in his arms. They held each other fast and rocked back and forth. Locked together, they performed loops and a figure eight, as if doing a dance of happiness.

Chen looked hardly more than thirty years old to Anna although she knew he was in his fifties. When Joe introduced her, she was almost knocked over by the force of his presence and the vitality of his glance. Truly he did seem like some sort of superman—or man-God. She could swear there was a halo of light not just around his head but around his entire person. He wore a simple outfit of white linen, loose pants, and shirt. His hair, thick, bright, and shiny, fell to his shoulders. His features were simple yet somehow stunning in their symmetry.

He exclaimed, "Joe, you look wonderful."

Did Joe? Anna wondered. Yes. He had looked enormously improved all day and now, aglow from the reunion, he seemed to have shed his years and his illness. Still, Anna had the feeling he was drawing with all his might on the life and strength left in him, that he was somehow creating new energy from the slim reservoir within or from the energy she and his teacher were bestowing upon him.

"This is a happy day for me," The Teacher went on. "And I thought I had got beyond all possible surprises. But, Joe, you were always a trickster. You always did the unexpected thing." Anna was again bowled over, this time by his voice. It was so soft that one's ears pricked to hear it, yet it penetrated right to the soul, by-passing the ears, and there was a tremolo to it so that it was more like singing than talking.

"Is he still a trickster, Anna? During those wonderful years when Joe and I were together and people came to follow us, he had a way of tricking them into illumination. He would answer a question for them and you could actually see a little light bulb go on over their heads." The Teacher laughed merrily. Anna laughed too; it was so contagious. "The only trouble was, then they would go away. They wouldn't need us any more. It was a good thing when Joe left me. Then my followers would stick around for a while and do some serious following." He laughed again and Joe and Anna laughed with him.

"Yes, he is still a trickster," Anna replied, particularly remembering the gold coins that flowed from Joe's fingers only two nights ago or, more importantly, how he greeted the pilgrims at the hermitage door in the guise of a servant.

"Can you both squeeze into my car? I'll give you the grand tour."

There was a space behind the seats where Anna could crouch and Joe took the passenger seat.

The next half hour they were whirled through the Universe-city, the students bowing as Chen passed them by—and many of them having to scurry out of the way for the sake of life and limb but, Anna thought, since death was proscribed, it would probably be okay if The Teacher ran them over. It wouldn't even leave tire tracks.

Despite his charismatic presence, her clouded feelings about him were not dispelled. Distrust prevailed, and every time she looked at Joe's glowing face she felt mystified.

Lost in her thoughts about Joe and his teacher, she hardly heard the spiel about all the different buildings and their purposes. She could see it was a wondrous place, laid out gracefully, the buildings modern, of pastel colors, complemented by rows of trees, gardens, parks, sculptures, fountains, amphitheaters.

He said he had a thousand students. "I will introduce you to them tonight. We will have a special gathering, for you are my first student and, at seventy-three, you are like a man in his prime. You epitomize all my ideas, Joe. And isn't it true that the whole world comes to see you? Aren't you the holy man?"

"No, I am still just the trickster," Joe said.

31
THE GOOD
TRICK

The Teacher's house was elegantly simple, the kind of simplicity that comes from the best designers with the best materials at the highest prices. It was modern, light, and airy, everything up-to-the-minute, spacious, restrained, yet colorful and even cozy. It was perfect, Anna thought. As was the meal—tasty and healthy and not overabundant. The wine was nectar. Students assiduously served them but were treated by The Teacher with politeness and respect. Joe accepted all offerings with pleasure but actually ate little, if at all, and drank nothing.

Anna felt it would be unfair to say it was all a disgusting display of wealth, but she thought that it was.

No more so than the president of any university or than any bishop of a church and yet . . . and yet . . . this was Joe's teacher whom he'd found as a boy in a monastery. Why was Joe not appalled at this life he led now—this inhumane anti-life which denied both birth and death?

Anna smiled to herself since it was she, not Joe, who was luxuriating at table. Her plate was clean, her wine glass empty. And soon there would be coffee!

Joe excused himself to go to his room. He asked to be called when he was wanted for "the Gathering."

A half hour later, as Anna stood with Joe in the wings, waiting for him to go on stage with his teacher, he asked Anna to bring him a chair. "Chen will go on for some time telling them what a phenomenon I am."

Anna returned with the chair and Joe asked her to place it on the stage where he could be seen. "I know Chen wants me to make my entrance doing cartwheels, but I must sit down now."

The holy man looked into Anna's eyes with ineffable sweetness and kissed her on the brow. She waited for what he would say, but he remained silent.

As Joe kissed Anna's brow, he thought to himself what a fierce-looking brow it was and how, before this day was done, it would grow black like a thundercloud.

Anna had been a very bad wise woman today. Sometimes, to

see her frowning at Chen, or rolling her eyes in exasperation, he'd had to stifle his laughter. Of course, Anna was still a mere wise-woman-in-training, quite rough about the edges, but nevertheless far ahead of others in her kindness and wisdom—evolved, and highly conscious.

A kaleidoscope of images of their journey swept across the holy man's mind—his favorite image being the one of her sitting on the airport floor, wrathfully tugging off her boots to give to the thief.

Last night, when he had awakened to feel her warm body clasping his, he'd thought it was fifty years ago. He had sat up to look to her other side for their little daughter. Then he had remembered where he was. It was Anna sleeping beside him, and he was the old holy man. But for the first time the loneliness of half a century was lifted from him because of her kindness and compassion.

Anna, too, would know loneliness in the years to come. She would have moments of black despair but, time and again, the darkness would dissolve in the light of understanding until it would come to her—the light and love that surpassed understanding.

Joe sat down, his body feeling glad of the chair. Now his mind was without thoughts or images. He smiled and closed his eyes. He heard Chen's sonorous voice, then nothing. He saw a gleaming whiteness waving and glimmering in his consciousness until it resolved into the form of the hermitage. It was not a memory. He was there in the boulder garden. How very nice. The boulders were white, too, as they appeared sometimes when the moonlight shone on them. Through the window he could see the monks at dinner. Astonished, they rose from the table as one and came to the window. There was the shining of eyes, smiles, rocks, stars. All, for the holy man, was radiance. All.

The Teacher stood before his thousand students and his soft clear voice spun from his mouth like silk from a cocoon, enchanting everyone. He told them about Joe and how, as his first student, he stood here now as the culmination of all his teachings—all that was good, wise, and immortal.

Anna did not ever think she would feel embarrassed for Joe, but she did now and bent her head in shame. It was as if The Teacher were making a circus act of the holy man, making him his own creature to perform at his command. And Joe was letting him.

He went on for some time, but finally he finished, saying, "Now it is time for you to hear from the holy man in his own words, and so I give you Joe, he who is the embodiment of truth."

Standing aside, he gestured gracefully to Joe, who remained sitting in the chair—remained sitting, and sitting.

Anna left her place in the wings, walked uncertainly over to Joe, and bent over him. She straightened up and looked over at

Chen. "He's dead." She spoke softly but everyone heard. There was a cumulative gasp, then a restless stirring and murmuring, a sense among them of ultimate horror.

The Teacher came over to Joe and only Anna heard him say, "That was a very good trick, Joe. It's too bad you can't see the light bulb over my head. But I guess you don't need to, do you?"

32
GRIEF

Anna fell apart. "We must get him off this horrible stage," she cried. She became strident and commanding. "No, don't send for your students. I forbid it. No strangers. We must carry him ourselves. We, whom he knew and loved." With superhuman strength she lifted the holy man in her arms. Carrying him from the stage, back toward The Teacher's house, staggering and lurching, she gasped out more orders. "We must lay him out comfortably and bathe him and I must wash his robe," she said. "There must be candles," she said. "Music. We'll sit with him through the night." It was as if by thinking of many things she could to do for Joe's body she could make what had happened not have happened. She could roll back time, and she and Joe could still be sitting together by the wall.

Chen remained silent. Before she crashed and fell, he took Joe's body from her and carried him forth effortlessly, no change in his light graceful stride. Anna still talked, no longer in ringing commands but more like a small burbling wail. "Oh, that he should die in this terrible place, that he should leave his beloved mountain and hermitage and monks to come to you."

"Yes," Chen said.

"I don't understand it. He said you were sick, that he needed to be by your side."

"Did he?"

"But he was the sick one. So sick. In pain. Suffering. He barely held himself together to get here. One night . . . why, it was only last night, he almost died. I wanted to take him to the hospital, but he said no, tomorrow he would be with you."

Chen hastened his steps and Anna trotted after him, calling in a despairing voice, "Why? Why? You are not worth it," tasting bitterness in her mouth, seeing red behind her eyes. "You are not worth it," she said cruelly.

Then they were back in his house, and Joe was placed on the bed that was to have been his for the night.

"I guess Joe thought that I was worth it," Chen said gently, turning to face Anna, bathing her with his eyes. "He honored me with his death. He came to remind me of death, because he is right. I am sick and he had to shock me out of it in the best way

113

that he could. He saved his dying for me to be at and take heed of. Do you understand?"

At last, Anna burst into tears. They streamed from her eyes. "But he is gone!" she cried. "He's gone!" And that's all she could say before her nose and throat became hopelessly clogged.

"No he's not, Anna. He's only transformed. He's gone to another existence."

"Joe didn't believe that," Anna said, using her kerchief to blow her nose and wipe her face, beginning to calm down.

"I do. And as long as we exist he will be in our hearts. Don't feel lonely. Don't feel abandoned." He took poor Anna into his arms and held her close. Unexpectedly, she felt soothed. "He gave you that beautiful last kiss. I saw him. Do you remember the kiss? It was his goodbye, you know."

Anna smiled with quivering lips. "And his eyes. You never saw such sweetness." Again she was overcome but recovered. "Chen, please forgive me. I have said unpardonable things. How disappointed Joe would be to have witnessed my abominable behavior. From the very start of this day he asked me to be serene, to be silent. No thinking, no talking, he said. But I didn't follow his advice for one minute. I have committed bad thoughts all day and now bad action, unspeakable action."

"Of course I forgive you."

114   "You see, everything you stood for seemed contrary to Joe's way, and therefore repugnant to me. I couldn't understand why he had come."

"Do you understand now?"

"Because he believed in you. He said you were a prophet. To the last, you were his beloved teacher. He always spoke of you with reverence."

"That is generous of you to say. Anna, don't feel bad about yourself. Naturally you were unbalanced by this day. Joe knew what he would find here, my sickness. It was not the shock to him that it was to you."

"Yes. He said he would make you well. He was glad. Do you know what the first words were he said this morning?"

Chen smiled and thought for a moment. "I'll bet he said this will be a wonderful day."

Again Anna wept. By now her robe was soaking wet as if she'd been out in a rainstorm, and the kerchief she clutched in her hand was a sodden ball.

"Anna, we will sit with Joe's body tonight and then tomorrow we will take his body back to the hermitage together for his burial. We will be there the next day."

"How is that possible?"

"I have a private jet, of course." He released his merry laugh. "Can you forgive me?"

"Who am I to forgive anyone after the way I have acted?"

I am not a wise woman, she thought to herself hopelessly. I am not even close. I'm a . . . she searched for a word. She remembered how dreadfully she had carried on: seizing Joe's body, caterwauling away, then speaking so cruelly to Chen. Luckily Joe died before he saw my true colors. Or did he die in part to show me my true colors, to show me how far I have to go?

Chen said, "Anna, whenever you are feeling bad about yourself, remember Joe's kiss of compassion. Remember he loved you not only for your wisdom but for your human-ness."

"I'm neither a wise woman nor a human, I'm a calamity," Anna said woefully, and then, wonderfully, incredibly, when he laughed at her remark, she laughed, too. They sat by Joe's dead body, laughing.

33
LYING

Always leave them laughing,' he said."
Anna was telling Chen about Joe's last visit with the children in the park. She and Chen were on the private jet. The chairs rotated so they faced each other as they talked. The chairs also collapsed into lounges so Anna could lie full length, which she intended to do very soon, exhausted from the night of sitting with Joe's body, sore at heart from her loss, feeling alone and disoriented, Joe no longer with her, Joe no longer in the world at all. Gone, forever gone.

She longed for sleep. Chen was one of those people who could sleep for five minutes and get energized for another eight hours.

The holy man's body was now in a casket, which was with them in the passenger part of the plane. Of course there were no casket makers in Universe-city, but The Teacher had ordered one of his student-handymen to bang one together and it was nice.

Anna remembered Joe's teaching that when a loved one dies you don't lose him, you give him back. She told herself, I have given Joe back, but she found no comfort in this. She tried: I have given Joe. I have given. I have. I.

When there was nothing in her mind, not even the I, especially not the I, she began to feel some comfort.

But now Chen was asking Anna to tell about their three-day trip in detail. He didn't seem to want to know anything about the twenty-five years since he'd seen Joe, nothing about the hermitage, the monks, the pilgrims, the life, or the wisdom, only the trip.

She'd only got as far as picking up Joe in the taxi. "Then he showed me how to wiggle my ears and cross my eyes at the same time and recommended that I practice until I had it down."

"I don't believe a woman can wiggle her ears."

"That's a ridiculous thing to say." Anna was deeply offended but also had to laugh at being offended about such a silly thing as ear-wiggling. She remembered that Joe, too, had suggested it was not normally within a woman's powers. Obviously the two men had discussed it sometime during their fifteen years together.

"Can you wiggle your ears?" she asked, not in a challenging way but simply curious to know.

"Yes."

She waited for him to display the talent, but he did not sweep away the slick black curtain of hair to show the good work that his ears could do. She began to feel he was lying. But why would one lie about such a thing as ear-wiggling? Why lie about anything, for that matter? Anna had never understood lying and why some people felt the necessity for it. It was so much easier to tell the truth. Why sow confusion?

But on this major subject of ear-wiggling, it seemed to her that you simply went ahead and did it if you could, like the taxi driver, Ezla, who had showed his stuff immediately when the subject came up. One didn't maintain a stance about it, saying he could do it, lying.

"Why aren't you going on with your story?" Chen asked.

"I am wondering why you are lying to me about your ear-wiggling."

He laughed. "It wasn't exactly a lie, since in the same breath I vowed to learn this arcane art of Joe's."

"Don't you think it would be better to vow to love little children, since the arcane art will be for their benefit?"

"Perhaps you are right. But then"—he paused thoughtfully in a way that left one hanging on his words even more—"will I have to vow to love grown-ups as well?"

"Good heavens! Don't you love people at all?"

119

"I love nature, beautiful things, art, literature, ideas. I particularly love this airplane. I loved Joe and one or two others."

"Well," Anna said grumpily, "learn to wiggle your ears. You might as well begin somewhere." Anna adjusted her chair and closed her eyes.

"Begin to be Joe, do you mean? No, Anna, it is not who or what you are. It is that you know who and what you are."

And not lie, Anna thought.

"Whereas lying," he said, "or not lying, is not important."

34
NOT LYING

Anna dreamed of Jimmy and Melissa and awoke feeling happy, feeling blessed. Soon she would hold them in her arms.

Chen was sitting on the floor of the plane in the lotus position, and so he remained for another three hours.

They were served a meal by the flight attendant, and then The Teacher continued his interrogation of Anna about the holy man's journey. In response, she told about the taxi ride to the airport, the crippled women, the thief, and the car crash.

"So you learned to always leave them laughing, and then what lesson did you take from the exchange with the collector?"

"To be creative," Anna said after a little thought. "To create, not accumulate."

"And from the crippled women you learned to ask for help when you need it."

"From the thief I learned not to cherish anything but to give away gladly. From the car crash I learned about taking the blame. But don't forget the first lesson of the trip was Joe's exchange with the holy bodyguard: to approach one's travels with the perception that men have holiness within, not evil, and yet to be attentive, mindful, because allowing yourself to be protected by another only hampers attentiveness and renders you half alive—not to mention drawing attention to yourself."

Even as she spoke, two bodyguards sturdily sat in the rear of the plane.

"This teaching trip was for you, not me," Chen said. He and Anna locked eyes.

"You're the one asking the questions," Anna replied. "I'm only telling you what you want to know."

"But I am asking the questions for your sake," he said, "to be sure you didn't miss anything."

Anna waited and asked herself if he was lying again. The answer was no. And this was no simple matter of ear-wiggling. This was major. For although Joe had told her at the outset it was to be a teaching trip, she'd forgotten it. Things happened. A lot happened as it turned out. But she'd been so wrapped up in Joe and in the traveling with him and concern for him that she wasn't thinking of lessons. Now Joe's teacher seemed almost to be suggesting Joe had conjured all the experiences for her sake. And truly, now that she thought about it, now that he made her think about it, the trip was riddled with lessons.

Anna next told Chen about the cafe and the men there who wanted her to come with them so that they could rape her and what Joe had done to effect their escape.

"I guess I learned that men in a mob are no longer holy and while I still mustn't hate my enemies, I must be prepared to outwit them and then to run like hell.

"I think the hardest part of the entire trip, though, was sitting on the train and listening to your future student talk about you and your ideas. Joe had instructed me to be still. I was to be silent and not judge. I was not even to think. Serenity was to be the keynote. This was impossible. But I have already told you about that, haven't I?"

Anna paused. "It sounds like some adventure was happening every minute, but actually most of the time Joe and I were together in silence, in peace, and in love."

"Which is what in-between-time has to be filled with to ready you for life and its difficulties," Chen said.

"Peace and love aren't in-between-time. It is the trouble that comes in between."

"Well, yes, you're right. And usually trouble only comes if you're looking for it."

"But we weren't looking for it!"

"Joe was. So he could teach you. Now he has prepared you well for a life of wandering."

123

"Wrong again," Anna said firmly. "My life is to be in the hermitage. A life of peace, silence, and love. I'm sorry, but I really do think this teaching trip was for you. The whole trip was for you. Won't you take it to heart?"

"Sorry," he replied, shocking her. "I have no heart."

"You are too hard on yourself." She smiled. "Maybe so I'll stop being so hard on you."

"I am incredibly easy on myself," he said, closing his eyes, his face like a beautiful impenetrable stone carving. But she didn't think he was sleeping, not even for five minutes. He seemed so lonely. Her heart went out to him.

Then Anna had a strange feeling that Chen had closed his eyes so as not to show how his heart went out to her.

35
GREED

They had flown through a day and a night, stopping once to refuel. Now it was dawn.

Anna was eating fruit, drinking coffee. "Awhile back, you spoke of the importance of knowing oneself, not to delude oneself, or pretend. What about greediness? Isn't that the worst of all? It seems to me that it is greed that leads to corruption, murder, war. Greed engenders all the other poisons."

Chen replied calmly, "It is because you are so upset about Joe's death that you keep attacking me. And so I submit to you that my love for my beautiful Universe-city and for this marvelous machine that carries us to our destination, tearing holes through the sky, is exactly the same as your attachment to your cowboy boots."

Anna was silent.

"And, if pressed, I would give them up just as easily as you were prepared to give up your boots to the thief."

"What would constitute your being pressed?" Anna asked wryly.

"I guess it would have to be something as powerful as preserving Joe's locket from the thief's covetousness." He paused and said thoughtfully, "Despite Joe's trick, I still believe in my ideas, my search for the immortality that the ancient Tao masters enjoyed, but I see that I was trying to continue life while at the same time denying life. Henceforth: birth, death, sickness, and old age will be honored at my Universe-city."

"Are you afraid of death?"

"I have put myself in the way of it a hundred times and it won't have me. This has encouraged my feeling of being an immortal and of wanting to pass on my practice to others."

Anna felt his sincerity, bizarre though his belief was, but she knew that was what made such gurus seductive. Their belief in their rightness, in their infallibility, combined with their golden tongues, was what created their charisma and drew disciples to them.

She said, "Everything, without exception, dies—the fruit fly in twenty-four hours, the giant redwood tree in two thousand years. We humans get a hundred years, tops. That's the arrangement. Possibly we go on to another life or come back to live another life here, but this is our only life for certain, and Joe's idea is to live this one in the kindest, wisest way we can, with the awareness of impermanence enhancing each day." Chen was silent. Anna felt embarrassed at her preachiness. "Well, then, back to greediness . . ."

"Yes. Greediness. Having is not greediness. Wanting is. Let us return to your boots."

"Must we?"

He laughed and continued. "If you wanted ten pairs of boots, if you were unable to eradicate the ongoing desire for more and more boots, you would be greedy. As long as we keep to our one pair, our one private jet plane, and our one city, we will not be poisoned. Therefore, please stop me, Anna, if I buy another plane."

"Surely you are not being serious."

"I am!"

"Chen, tell me, please, how many cars do you have?"

"I have a fleet of cars," he admitted. He then added, laughing, "But it is only one fleet."

Anna no longer found his laugh contagious. "You are deluded," she said. "It is part of your sickness."

Chen looked thoughtful.

36
THE
HOLY MAN

They were nearing their destination. The plane had begun its descent, whispering powerfully through the air. Anna explained to Chen that the limousine he had arranged to meet them would be useless because, once in the town, they would have to walk the ten steep miles to the hermitage.

"I will have my men arrange for a stretcher. The casket will be too bulky to carry. I laid Joe on yards and yards of white linen, the same linen my shirts are made from. We can wrap him in the cloth before putting him on the stretcher." As he talked, he crouched down by the casket and seemed to have the intention of opening it. Upset, Anna turned away. "Come, Anna, we may as well prepare him now."

Anna did not want to come. As a nurse she had seen many people die, but she had not seen them almost three days dead. Nor did she want to view Joe that way, when putrification would have set in. She wanted to remember him as he looked when he kissed her brow, and as he was the night of his death, seeming to be sleeping peacefully.

But as Chen raised the lid, she exclaimed at the delicate scent that flowed forth into the pressurized cabin. "Why, it is Joe's favorite spring flower—the mountain lupin, blue as the sky. How were you able to find them in your agricultural valley?"

"Come here, Anna," Chen urged her. "Come and see."

Reluctantly, she left her chair.

Joe lay in his wheat-colored robe on the many folded lengths of white linen, uncorrupted, still looking beautiful, restful, at peace, the lovely aroma of mountain lupin caressing the air all around him—only there were no flowers.

37
THE NEW
ORDER

At the airport, the two bodyguards carried the casket, Anna her pack, and Chen his luggage. The limousine was awaiting them. So were the three crippled women. The blind one had a brightly colored kerchief folded narrowly and tied over her unsightly eyes. The armless one wore the kerchief around her neck, and the shrivelled-legged one wore hers around her waist. She handed Anna the bundle of kerchiefs Joe had ordered. "I hope you don't mind that we took three for ourselves."

"Of course not. I am delighted. You all look so cheerful!"

Chen said, "This means you are now members in good standing of the holy order of Annakerchiefians, the motto of which is, 'It's good luck to be nice.' Wear them with joy."

Anna turned wondering eyes upon Chen.

"Joe told me about it. I guess he neglected to tell you."

"You did not need to tell us," said the blind woman. "We could see at once what was happening. Our holy man is gone, but the wise woman has come to stay. Anna, we are proud of you, and these kerchiefs are flags of your wisdom. In fact, now that I am wearing this kerchief, I feel a lot more aware."

"We all feel better," said the armless one, "but I still feel the phantom pain in my arms."

Anna felt shy about laying her hands on the woman's stubs, especially in front of Chen, since all her life she'd been so careful to keep her healing powers hidden, but she fluttered her fingers against the stubs and along the arms and hands that were no longer there. It was all done in the blink of an eye, and the next minute she was climbing into the limousine where Joe's casket was already waiting.

Chen joined her a few minutes later, having first ascertained from the women where to find a stretcher. He directed the chauffeur to the hospital and the stretcher was soon installed in the car. Then Anna said, "First let's take the kerchiefs to the children in the park because Joe promised."

The children came running when they saw the limousine, for this was not a normal sight in the town. Anna got out, introducing herself. "I am Anna. I've come to bring the kerchiefs Joe promised you." She distributed the colorful squares, and there were exactly the right amount of them—as if they kept reproducing with the approach of each child. Some of the children adorned themselves while others ran around, holding them in their hands, letting the cloth fly out behind them like banners.

"Wear them with joy," Anna quoted Chen, whom she noticed had got out of the car and was standing nearby. "And remember, it's good luck to be nice."

One of the older children translated for the others, then solemnly asked, "Did Joe die?"

"Yes, he did," Anna said, but seeing the face begin to crumple, she quickly added, "He would not want you to be sad about it. He loved nothing so much as the sound of your laughter."

The boy said, as a most wonderful eulogy, Anna thought, "Joe was funny."

"Yes, he was very funny."

"What else did Joe say?"

"He once told me that when he died he didn't need to go to heaven because he went to heaven every time he came to play in the park." Anna was talking to Chen as well as the children, for it seemed she would persist in trying to teach the unteachable teacher. "He was always learning from you. How to be relaxed and take time, how to be open, curious, unrestrained and, most especially, how to play. And, do you know what? My two little children came to live at the hermitage, so he got to have children with him before he died."

"And hear them laugh?"

"Yes. And, of course, cry, too, which is another sound of life. Now I must hurry home to Melissa and Jimmy because I've been away from them for five whole days!"

"They came to play with us yesterday. With their dad."

"They did?" Anna was surprised and glad. She removed her kerchief from around her neck and waved it. "Goodbye."

"Goodbye," they all shouted in their language and in English. One after another, the children balled up the kerchiefs and threw them into the air where they opened and floated down like flying flowers.

38
THE
UNTHINKABLE

The limousine left them at the trail head where the lilac still bloomed as it had at the beginning of Anna and Joe's journey. Joe, wrapped in the snowy linen, was placed on the stretcher and they began the ascent, Chen and the two body-guards taking the four handles, Anna leading the way, past the sorrowful wooden sign with the carved words: THE HOLY MAN IS GONE.

After a small distance, she hesitated, saying, "There was something else Joe wanted me to do in the town, but I've forgotten."

"It will come to you," said Chen, and it came back to Anna at once as if summoned by him.

"He told me he had an errand to do at the photographer's shop and that I was to pick it up upon my return."

"It will wait. You will remember it next time."

The sun went behind some clouds and a drizzly rain began to fall. A rainbow appeared briefly, then disappeared behind a curtain of more serious rain. Their trek began to assume the guise of a mournful funeral procession, heads bent so as to place their feet carefully. The trail was muddy and as it grew steeper it ran with water, so they sloshed miserably along. The weather passed in a half hour and the sun came out, attended by bird song. The spring flowers shook off the rain and opened before their very eyes, releasing heady aromas into the swept air, attracting a population of honey bees that joined the procession.

Only a quarter of the way along, they took a break, sitting on a boulder, drying their clothes and enjoying the view that seemed to stretch through time as well as distance. The bees sought out clover. The bodyguards, with their previously impassive, almost brutal faces, now were relaxed and smiling. They brought out packets of sandwiches to eat, then lay back, soaking up the sun, apparently deciding not to be ready to give their lives for Chen for the next couple of minutes. Chen remained attentive and Anna restlessly wished they would get going again. The closer she got to home, the more excited she was to see her family. 135

Chen stood up, hearing and seeing Kim before Anna did a

few minutes later. The young monk arrived on the run. "I have been looking for you every hour," he said, "running the trail." He nodded a greeting to the men, then looked at Anna gravely, his face distressed. He noticed the stretcher with Joe's body wrapped in white linen, sprinkled with a golden scattering of bees. Anna started to speak, but he said, "It's all right. We know that Joe is dead. We knew to the minute. And we have prepared the ground. But there is something else . . ."

"Kim, will you run back and tell the children I'm here. Maybe they could come to meet me."

"Anna." Kim spoke with difficulty, brow creased with pain. "Errol took them to town yesterday and has not returned."

"The children in the park said they came to play yesterday. Errol probably decided to spend a night before the long walk home." Anna looked at Kim, not understanding his concern.

"Jacob followed Errol to town but lost him. He looked for him everywhere, but he was not at any of the inns. Jacob is not far behind me. He can tell you . . ."

Now it hit Anna that they thought Errol had stolen the children away, had left the country with them. She closed her eyes. Red and orange flashed in her brain, as if it had caught fire and she would never again be able to think. Or maybe the vivid flashing colors were protection so she would not have to think the unthinkable.

39
AWAKENING

Anna came to with her head in Chen's lap. His hand lay lightly on her brow. The searing colors were gone, but she felt deeply tired.

Chen said softly, "My men have gone on to the hermitage with the stretcher. Jacob and Kim are here."

Anna remembered the news Kim had greeted her with, but she took hope from Jacob's presence. Maybe Kim had got it wrong.

She sat up, leaning on Chen. "Jacob?"

"Hello, Anna. I'm so sorry. I was afraid Errol might leave in your absence, but I never thought he'd take the children. I followed him just in case. He told me he was going halfway down the mountain to see the ponies, but he went all the way to town.

They went to the park and played. Then I saw him get into the town taxi with Jimmy and Melissa. I commandeered a car but lost them."

"Did you go to the airport?" Anna asked fearfully.

"I did. They weren't there. I stayed until the only plane left." Anna took heart. "That's good."

"Then I went to all the inns, but no luck."

"We have to find Ezla, the taxi driver," Anna said positively. "He will know where they went." She stood up and Chen stood, too. "Chen, I'll go back to the town with Jacob. Kim will show you the way to the hermitage. I'm sure I'll rejoin you by tonight but, well, my children must come before everything, before Joe's funeral, before the hermitage . . ."

"Yes."

She might not find her family in the town. She thought of what Chen had said about the meaning of her journey with Joe preparing her for a life of wandering. She felt frightened. With enormous effort, Anna controlled her fear.

"You must be so tired, Anna," Kim said.

"We can start first thing in the morning," Jacob said, assuming as a matter of course that he would accompany her.

"We must go right now, Jacob."

"Yes," Chen said again. He put his hands lightly on her shoulders. They burned through her robe and skin. She felt a jolt of new energy from his touch. Her fatigue fell away from her. "It is a time for utter fearlessness," he said. Anna remembered Joe saying that fearlessness was not bravery or courage, it was calmness. But she did not feel calm. Her mind was whirling, her body in a fight or flight mode.

She turned to Kim. "There was so much I wanted to tell you. But Chen knows the whole story. He got it out of me, every word." She wondered again about Chen's interrogation and the things he had said about it. But it was a time for action, not for thinking. She must not think backward or forward. Her mind must be free to concentrate on the search for her children. And she must keep within her an ever-hopeful heart. But her mind still whirled and her nerves were jangled. She could not even see straight.

She must have closed her eyes again. When she opened them, Kim and Chen were proceeding up the trail, talking eagerly together, looking, Anna thought, like father and son or like two brothers, and she felt glad for them both that through giving back Joe they had met each other. They seemed full of light to her while she stood in darkness, alone, without Joe, the monks, or her family. It was just she and Jacob again. They had met in the line, fellow pilgrims. He had come to Ireland to return her to Joe and had stayed on, anointing himself her protector. They were friends to the death.

She thought back to a week ago, watching the sunset with Melissa on her lap, Jimmy standing beside her with an arm around her neck, Joe sitting on the other side—and felt overwhelmed with a sense of loss.

From here the shining white hermitage was not in sight. Perhaps it was just as well not to glimpse it and wonder when, if ever, she would return to reside within its happy walls.

Chen turned and called back to her, "Don't forget your errand in the town."

The words awakened her. She picked up her pack, which Jacob took from her and put on his back, and turned to face the downward trail, telling herself that soon she would hold her children in her arms. She must keep a clear, untroubled mind. She must travel the path before her without longing or fear.

The darkness lifted from Anna and the mountain landscape was illuminated. The air tasted fresh in her mouth. The world was wondrous in her sight—the rocks, trees, grasses, and sky!

"Let's go!" She started down the trail, almost running, Jacob plunging after her with great strong steps.

40
EZLA'S GIFT

Anna and Jacob raced back to town but then stood bewildered in the town square, not knowing how to proceed, since there was no sign of Ezla or his taxi. They asked around but got no satisfaction. Then, to her enormous relief, she saw the three disabled women inching through the crowd, the blind woman pulling the cart of the legless woman while tied to the armless one, who was leading the way.

Anna hailed them and explained her difficulty. "My husband and children seemed to have disappeared into thin air. They were last seen yesterday, getting into Ezla's taxi."

"We haven't seen Ezla all day. Many times he takes off to go pot-collecting, leaving hopeful customers stranded, missing appointments and planes. This town really needs another taxi. We would take over his business, but it would be difficult in our condition."

They wanted to discuss the pros and cons of being taxi drivers and did not seem to understand, as Anna did, that it was absolutely out of the question, not worth considering at all. Even if they could all sit on top of each other it would not work. She tried to be patient and polite but finally interrupted, crying, "Ezla isn't going to collect pots anymore. Can you please tell me where he lives?"

They told Anna where to find his house on the outskirts of town, and she and Jacob hastened in the direction they pointed.

Rounding a curve, they came upon Errol, Melissa, and Jimmy heading their way, down the muddy, puddle-strewn road.

In the joyful commotion of greeting, Anna wept tears of joy and relief. Everyone talked at once except for Jacob, who stood aside. Mostly the children wanted to show her the pots they had made at Ezla's. "That's why we've been so long," Jimmy said. "We had to wait for them to be fired."

"We slept at Ezla's," Melissa said. "His house is full of pots. It's a pot house."

"We were going to the airport to meet you," said Jimmy, "but Ezla said there weren't any planes and took us to his house instead and showed us how to make pots. Look at Dad's."

Errol had made a truly beautiful pot. "It's for you," he said. "A present."

The children chattered away while kissing her, tugging at her clothes, crawling into her arms, almost trying to get inside her.

"I heard about Joe," Errol said when he could get a word in. "I'm sorry. Are you all right, Anna?"

"I am now. Yes. I'm all right." She looked into his eyes. Had he really gone to the airport to meet her? Or was it to leave her? He looked back at her steadily, clear-eyed.

She knew there had been an outgoing plane yesterday because Jacob had waited for it to take off. But Ezla had told Errol there were no planes—perhaps saving her family for her with this lie. She would not ask Errol for the truth of it. She would believe in him and in their love. What was the good of a marriage if there was no trust? She knew he'd been upset about life in the hermitage and, in her absence, he could have made a rash decision to leave. If so, he had only half-acted upon it. He had not left. He was here now and they all looked so happy with their hand-made pots. She was happy, too. Even the ever-sorrowful Jacob looked happy.

For the first time since Joe's death Anna grasped how life went on, didn't stop for a minute. In the few days since his death she'd experienced so much—love and laughter, anger and black despair—and she'd discovered the strength that was in her—that she could go on and do what she had to do, come what may. Maybe Joe hadn't made such a bad choice after all. A vision of the floating kerchiefs came to her eyes.

"Shall we be on our way up the mountain?" Errol said. She was so glad he'd been the one to say it.

"Yes."

"I'll go for the ponies," Jacob said.

"We'll meet at the trail head," said Anna. "I have a quick errand to run first."

41
JOE'S GIFT

At the photography store, Alim, the man whose ambition had once turned the town against him so that he'd run angrily up the mountain to blame Joe, then stayed to be a monk, greeted Anna. "Hello, Anna, I've been expecting you." He had the bright, calm, clear-eyed countenance of the enlightened.

"You've heard about Joe?" Anna asked gently.

"Yes. We are all so sad about Joe's death. He was one in ten thousand million. The whole town will come to his funeral, those of us who can put one foot in front of the other. I bet the dappled ponies will come, too, and even the warrior ghosts who play the game. The boulder birds will gather on the hermitage rocks to sing a requiem for Joe, and I would be unsurprised if the mountain wildflower flocks find some way to uproot themselves and make an appearance. Meanwhile, Joe's monks from all over the world are flying here for the service."

"He has left the world a better place, Alim."

"True. Everyone I know who has been in contact with him now tries to treat other men and women as holy persons, being courteous, and thoughtful, and kind. It is so easy! And what a payback!"

"Did Joe leave something here for me?"

"Yes. It is a present for you from Joe. It is not for the hermitage, although it is his official portrait."

He handed her a small picture framed in gold-painted wood, covered in glass. It showed Joe in a pencil drawing, all head and ears and lopsided eyes, spidery arms, legs, hands, and feet, tilted on the paper, as if flying. In Joe's printing was written: "The Holy Man, 1923–1996, by Melissa."

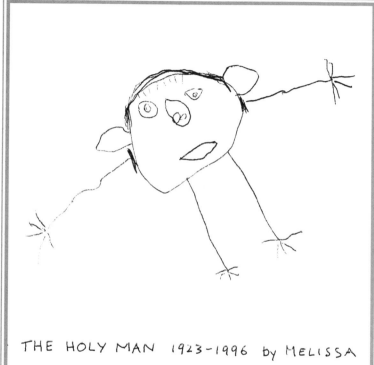

THE HOLY MAN 1923-1996 by MELISSA

ABOUT THE AUTHOR

Susan Trott is the author of ten previous novels.
She lives in northern California.